"Talk to me, Sierra. What do you want to happen between us?"

Could she claim a night for herself with him? The idea had smoked around the edges of her thoughts for days, tempting her. Teasing her.

"I don't want to risk my chance to spend time with Micah," she found herself saying.

"I would never do that to him. Or you." The sincerity in his voice rang true. "You've been a constant in his life, and he doesn't have enough of those."

She appreciated hearing that Colt saw her that way. That he respected the bond she'd developed to his son.

"Thank you. He means a lot to me." Leaning into Colt's touch, she allowed herself the pleasure of his strong hands on her. Her pulse quickened. Heat stirred inside her.

Was she really considering this?

* * *

The Rancher's Reckoning by Joanne Rock is part of the Texas Cattleman's Club: Fathers and Sons series.

Dear Reader,

For those of us who love romance, no two stories are ever alike. Every boy-meets-girl tale is special in its own unique way, and that's one of many reasons I'll never tire of hearing about the road to a couple's happily-ever-after.

Colt and Sierra's story is special to me because of their unlikely journey to become parents. Sierra has long tried to wrap her head around the idea of never being a mother, a hurt she's tried desperately to bury. I ached along with her as she reached out to help an abandoned child, putting her heart on the line all while knowing she might lose her connection to the baby she grew to love.

As for Colt, the guilt he feels in abandoning his child—unknowingly—is devastating. I loved that the woman who found his baby was the one who showed him how to be a father.

Every romance is different. And parenthood comes to us in different and unique ways, as well. With *The Rancher's Reckoning*, I'm celebrating those love stories, too!

Happy reading,

Joanne Rock

JOANNE ROCK

———

THE RANCHER'S RECKONING

Special thanks and acknowledgment are given
to Joanne Rock for her contribution to the
Texas Cattleman's Club: Fathers and Sons miniseries.

HARLEQUIN®
DESIRE™

Recycling programs
for this product may
not exist in your area.

ISBN-13: 978-1-335-73553-9

The Rancher's Reckoning

Harlequin Enterprises ULC
22 Adelaide St. West, 41st Floor
Toronto, Ontario M5H 4E3, Canada
www.Harlequin.com

Printed in U.S.A.

Joanne Rock credits her decision to write romance after a book she picked up during a flight delay engrossed her so thoroughly that she didn't mind at all when her flight was delayed two more times. Giving her readers the chance to escape into another world has motivated her to write over eighty books for a variety of Harlequin series.

Books by Joanne Rock

Harlequin Desire

Brooklyn Nights

A Nine-Month Temptation
Ways to Tempt the Boss
The Stakes of Faking It

Dynasties: Mesa Falls

The Rebel
The Rival
Rule Breaker
Heartbreaker
The Rancher
The Heir

Texas Cattleman's Club: Fathers and Sons

The Rancher's Reckoning

Visit her Author Profile page at Harlequin.com, or joannerock.com, for more titles.

You can also find Joanne Rock on Facebook, along with other Harlequin Desire authors, at Facebook.com/harlequindesireauthors!

To my mother. I love you, Mom.

One

Please respond. I think you might be the father of the late Arielle Martin's six-month-old baby.

Seated at the oak desk in her room at a bed-and-breakfast in Royal, Texas, investigative journalist Sierra Morgan reread the text she'd just composed.

Blunt?

Absolutely. And considering the negative stereotypes of journalists as relentless sensationalists who would do anything for a story, Sierra hated that this text played a little too close to that depressing portrayal. But she couldn't imagine any story more worthy of closure than that of a fatherless six-month-old.

Forcing herself to take an extra moment before clicking Send on the text, Sierra idly spun a yellowed globe from the early 1900s, her gaze moving over the stack of old leather-bound novels that served as a makeshift pedestal. She'd been staying at the Cimarron Rose for months to solve the mystery paternity of baby Micah, who'd been found abandoned in the parking lot of the Royal Memorial Hospital.

Sierra had just arrived in town to do a story for *America* magazine on the ten-year anniversary of the Texas Cattleman's Club allowing women into their ranks. She'd filed her story after the gala celebrating the TCC milestone, and freelanced several articles for the local *Royal Gazette*, but she hadn't been able to tear herself away from baby Micah's story. Yes, she was dogged and relentless and all those other things that made up a good reporter.

Better people thought that than the truth—that baby Micah tugged at her heartstrings for far more personal reasons.

She'd figured out who the baby's mother was soon enough once Micah's aunt woke up in the hospital after an untimely collapse. But even then, Eve Martin hadn't been able to shed any light on the mystery of Micah's father, because Eve's sister, Arielle, had died of a heart attack before naming the daddy. Since then, Sierra had been pursuing leads for five months with Arielle Martin's diary as her guide.

Now, Sierra spun in the desk chair, the afternoon light slanting through a window overlooking the lawn. A vintage map of the world sprawled above the four-poster bed, and a huge repurposed suitcase served as a chest at the foot of it. While she cooled her heels in Texas, somewhere on the other side of the globe, rancher Colt Black was revamping a French winery, ignoring all her more subtly worded texts and voice mails.

She truly believed she'd finally cracked the mystery of Micah's parentage. But she needed Colt Black to answer her in order to confirm it.

Grip tightening on her phone, she returned her gaze to the least tactful lines she'd ever composed.

Blunt and relentless? Color her guilty.

She jabbed the send button.

Because she knew how it felt to grow up with the knowledge that you'd been abandoned as a child. That was a lifelong wound she wouldn't wish on anyone, and Sierra felt deeply protective of the sweet six-month-old she'd visited many, many times since his arrival in Royal.

One way or another, Colt Black would have to answer her now.

Had a homecoming ever felt so hollow?

Colt Black didn't even look out the window of

the luxury SUV he'd hired at the airport as they drove through downtown Royal. He'd been away from Texas for fifteen months. Just twenty-four hours ago he would have guessed he'd feel some gladness to return to the Lone Star state after being in the Occitanie region of southwest France for over a year.

Not now.

He withdrew his cell phone from the pocket of his sports jacket to re-read the series of texts from the journalist Sierra Morgan. He'd never heard of the woman until he'd researched her last night after that final, devastating message.

Please respond. I think you might be the father of the late Arielle Martin's six-month old baby.

The words still made his chest seize up even on the hundredth read. Yes, he'd ignored all her other texts and voice mails leading up until that last bombshell. But that had been when he'd thought she was just a reporter sniffing out gossip for more articles for the local paper, the *Royal Gazette*.

Once Arielle Martin's name came up, however, he'd dropped everything else. Literally. He'd been in the winery's tasting room shortly before midnight, testing a competing vintage from a neighboring winemaker, when he'd read the words that gutted him.

Had he fathered a child without knowing?

Immediately, he'd gone back to read Sierra Morgan's other texts more carefully, only to discover Arielle had died one month after giving birth. And that her child—quite possibly *his* child, even though he'd only been with Arielle for one night—had been without a parent ever since. That had been five months ago.

If this child was his?

Colt wouldn't ever forgive himself.

Glancing up from his phone, he pocketed the device again as he saw the bed-and-breakfast come into view. The unassuming Cimarron Rose had been a Royal fixture for years, long before Natalie Valentine took it over and turned the downstairs into a bridal shop. In one of the journalist's messages, she had told him she had taken a room here, and she'd listed all her contact information for him to get in touch. Of course, he hadn't. Last night he'd been too devastated to call her for more details. Instead, he'd booked the first flight out to discover the truth for himself.

So here he was, showing up at her door unannounced at—he checked his watch, too jet-lagged to remember the local hour after crossing so many time zones—ten o'clock in the morning.

The SUV rolled to a stop on the gravel drive that wound under a porte cochere. The bright red roof and ivory exterior of the main building had a hospitable air with a wide porch and hanging ferns between every column. After paying the driver, Colt approached the wide front entrance, where the door had been left ajar, perhaps to let the mild breeze inside.

"Hello?" he said through the screen, rapping his knuckles lightly on the wooden door frame.

The scent of coffee and cinnamon preceded the sound of muted footsteps and a feminine voice.

"Come in," called a woman before she came into view. "Natalie's out, but I'm—"

A petite blonde beauty stopped as she opened the door wider and met his gaze.

Wide, moss green eyes stared up at him. Tousled, flaxen hair spilled over the shoulders of her black T-shirt with a picture of a coffee cup and the words Caffeinated Writer in swirling script. She wore a pair of pink-striped pajama pants with the tee and a pair of gray flannel slippers on her feet.

"You must be Sierra," he managed to say at last, suddenly aware of the moments that had passed while he took a far too detailed inventory of the woman. "I'm Colt Black."

She blinked at him, seeming to awaken from her own perusal. No doubt she was surprised. "You're *here*."

She probably thought him the world's biggest deadbeat for not replying to her messages before.

Or were her reporter instincts too busy salivating over the possibility of a local scoop?

"And well overdue, at that," he said dryly. Then, nodding at the screen door, he tugged it toward him, determined to keep his cool until he took her measure. "May I?"

Belatedly, she backed up a step to clear the way.

"Of course. Yes. I've been anxious to speak with you. Obviously. I just wasn't expecting you so soon after—" Her green gaze stuck to him while he stepped onto the dark welcome mat and set his leather overnight bag on a wooden hall bench. She seemed to regroup, and he suspected she made an effort to restrain the questions plainly written in her gaze. Instead, she asked, "Would you like some coffee? Tea?"

Sierra gestured to a small breakfast bar laden with pastries, a coffee machine, a kettle and a basket of tea bags. She retrieved her own mug, positioning it like a barrier between them, then took a careful sip while eyeing him over the rim.

"No, thank you. I'm wound up enough as it is between not sleeping and your text." He couldn't help the bite in his tone.

One eyebrow arched. "The fate of an infant seemed too important to waste any more time mincing words." Her green eyes blazed.

But was that defensiveness of the baby she felt? Or did that inner fire stem from a drive to nail down a story? If he didn't want to be the subject of her next feature, he needed to be on guard.

"You certainly came right to the point." He ground his teeth together as he peered around the front parlor room devoid of any guests save her. "Care to share what led you to me? And if I'm the subject of an article? I know you write for *America* magazine."

"Not currently, I don't." She shook her head. Then, gaze narrowing, she continued. "And although I freelance for the local paper, I'm not writing any more about Micah out of respect for Eve Martin and her nephew."

"There've already been stories about the baby." He'd Googled his way across the Atlantic. "So excuse me if I find that hard to believe."

"I wrote initially to drum up more leads to the father. But now I won't write anything else until I can report a happy ending, and only then with the father's permission. Today I'm interested in resolving a human drama because I was there when Micah was found."

Was she personally invested? The hint of accusation made him defensive.

"Well, I'm here now," he reminded her, needing to figure out if the child was his. "I'm ready to meet the boy. Talk to Arielle's family. Put the wheels in motion for an expedited DNA test—"

He had a to-do list a mile long, but Sierra settled

a hand on his forearm, startling him to silence with the unexpected touch.

"No one will be more supportive of moving quickly on this than me, but we should probably share what we know before you meet Micah." She seemed to realize she'd left her hand on his arm because she yanked it away quickly. Then she nodded toward a back door visible through a bright yellow-and-white kitchen. "Can we talk outside? I could use some air."

"Anywhere is fine," he said more tersely than he'd intended. "I just need answers. The sooner the better."

Bristling, she straightened her shoulders and set her coffee mug back on the buffet table.

"I have been trying to talk to you for *weeks*," she informed him levelly, folding her arms. "Before that, I spent months following leads from Arielle Martin's diary to locate Micah's father. So believe me, I am ready for answers, too."

It was on the tip of his tongue to say she should have tried harder to reach him. That if she'd sent that last text message two weeks ago, he would have been here that much sooner. But since he wouldn't even know that Arielle had given birth to a child without the woman standing before him, Colt reined himself in.

"Of course, you're right." His heart slammed in his chest, the angst of the last twenty hours wrecking his head. "Excuse my lack of manners, Miss Morgan. I'm furious with myself at the possibility that I left Arielle with no support…"

There were no words that could adequately describe his regret if that turned out to be the case. Accountability and responsibility could have been the Black family motto, drilled into him from an early age. The only thing that came a close second in importance was family itself. And that might be another institution Colt had denigrated by leaving the States fifteen months ago.

"I imagine it's a lot to process. Which is why I would have preferred to be less blunt in my text." Her tone was softer as she pivoted on her heel and started toward the kitchen. "Come on. Let's get some air. And please, call me Sierra."

Colt followed her through the kitchen, a flyer for a local Wine and Roses Festival snagging his gaze for an instant and capturing his professional interest as a newly minted French vintner. But with any luck he'd be back overseas before the event anyhow. He kept pace with Sierra down the back steps of the bed-and-breakfast onto a shaded lawn where an oak tree spread thick boughs over much of the space. A wrought iron bench sat between pink and purple azalea bushes already in bloom.

Sierra's slippers scuffed quietly against the flagstones as she moved toward the bench, her long blond hair blowing lightly against the middle of her back.

"Thank you." He waited for her to sit and then took the opposite end of the bench for himself. In the light breeze, he thought he caught a hint of her scent vying with the green shoots of a fresh Texas spring. "And to spare you time, I will tell you that I read everything I could find online related to Arielle's sudden death. I never met her sister, Eve, but it sounded like she was the guardian for her the baby?"

"Micah," Sierra corrected him, sounding oddly protective. "And yes, that's true. But Eve Martin was hospitalized with heart problems of her own until recently, and it was deemed best for Micah to remain in the care of Camilla Wentworth—Cammie—the woman who found him."

Colt felt ill at the thought of a total stranger acting as stand-in parent to an infant that might share Colt's blood.

"I need to see him." His hand tightened into a fist where it lay on the wrought iron. "My God, the boy deserves a home—"

"And he will find his rightful one." Sierra stabbed her finger against the bench to make the point. "But Cammie and Eve have trusted me to take on this search for Micah's father, allowing me to use Arielle's diary for any clues. So I would appreciate you sharing how you knew Arielle. I went out on a limb connecting the dots from her diary to suggest you could be the father."

"You didn't sound like you were making casual guesses in your text." He sat back to look at her.

Her lips compressed into a line before she spoke. "I did what needed to be done to find answers. Yet even after flying all the way here, you don't seem inclined to share how you knew Arielle."

Colt pressed a thumb to his temple. He didn't owe this woman the intimate details. He could simply walk away and find Cammie Wentworth on his own. Yet if there was anything to what Sierra said about her having the trust of the baby's guardian, perhaps it would be wisest to hash through this here with her before he got distracted meeting a child that might be his heir.

"Our time together was brief," he explained finally. "We met right before I left for France. I was devastated over the death of my grandfather and eager to begin work on a dream that was dear to him—opening a winery. I realize my grief is a poor excuse for being so careless as not to contact her afterward." He studied Sierra in the patchy sunlight that filtered through the tree overhead. "Do you know if anyone else made a claim for the—for Micah?"

"No one has," she admitted, sliding out of her slippers to tuck her feet under her. "But since Arielle's diary never mentioned you, I was basing my sleuthing work on really limited evidence."

Colt considered this. The ache of regret in his chest had expanded to a throbbing of urgency in his temples, blotting out the resentment he felt for Sierra's blunt insertion of herself into the drama. He needed to find out for certain if Micah was his son, and if Sierra could help him do that, so be it.

The news still staggered him.

His life would have to change drastically, starting immediately. Yet one thing was clear.

"In that case, I owe you a great debt for finding me, Sierra." He could set his personal feelings aside long enough to acknowledge that. "One I don't know how I'll ever repay."

Sierra stared into Colt Black's serious blue eyes, trying to get a feel for him.

Could she trust his account of meeting Arielle? DNA tests wouldn't lie, of course. And if he were the father, she'd obviously back off to allow the baby to reunite with his daddy. But until that was proven, Sierra felt obligated to run interference so that Cammie wasn't wasting her time playing host to a local rancher who might not be connected to Micah at all. And Eve had basically given up, thinking the father would never be found. She'd been working extra hard on her physical therapy, assuming she'd be raising Micah.

For now, Sierra planned to stick to Colt. Find out if he was a good person. A trustworthy person. The kind of man who would give Micah a good home.

Because it wasn't enough to be attractive. And she couldn't deny Colt was that. Her awareness of the fact came as a surprise, considering she had thought she'd successfully shut down that part of herself to focus on her career and forget about… other things.

Sure, Colt was tall and muscular. Imposing, almost, but that had more to do with his serious, intense demeanor. She understood logically that he was a very good-looking man. His tailored blue jacket and gray flannel pants broadcast his wealth as clearly as the vintage silver watch on his wrist. But the shadows under his eyes and the slight rumple of his freshly trimmed dark hair gave away how little he'd slept since learning the news. Those hints of his distress pulled at her more than his outward appearance since they might suggest he cared.

And then, Sierra found herself drawn to the determination in his expression. The need to make things right.

After the months of worrying about Micah's future, she found Colt's concern appealing.

The thought reminded her of his remark. That he felt indebted to her.

"You don't owe me anything." She swiped away

a dried leaf from the bench. "It will be reward enough if I can see Micah returned to family."

Although then she'd need to dig into her other mission in Royal. To write a book about the history of the Texas Cattleman's Club. Professionally, the project appealed to her. Personally, she couldn't help but take a deeper interest in Baby Micah. As much as she wanted to bring Micah together with his father, Sierra would miss her frequent visits to the child who'd found a spot in her heart.

"If Arielle never mentioned me in the diary, how did you end up finding out about me?" Colt swiped a hand through his hair.

"Arielle had jotted the name of the Colt Room in the margins of the diary," she explained, referencing the luxe bar inside the Texas Cattleman's Club that one of Colt's ancestors had founded and Colt himself had recently paid to renovate. "One of the references had a heart next to the name, so at first I thought she met the father of her child there."

Colt frowned, a line between his heavy, dark eyebrows. "That's not much to go on."

"But there was more. Micah's middle initial is C. No name, just a C. I thought all along it could be a nod to his father." Sierra had gone over and over that diary searching for clues, the mystery obsessing her for days on end.

"It's amazing you found me at all," he muttered darkly, rubbing a hand over his face. "I was so absorbed with the winery, needing to make it a success for my grandfather. And all the while I should have been here, making sure Arielle had everything she needed."

Sierra heard the despair and self-recrimination in his words. She wished she had a way to distract him since neither of those things would help the situation.

"You're here now though. And I have to admit, you moved quickly once I put my cards on the table." She slumped more deeply against the bench, drawing her knees to her chest to hug them to her. And maybe to add a barrier between her and the compelling man sitting beside her. "Once I researched more about the Colt Room and your involvement, combined with the fact that you left the country soon after Arielle became pregnant, I thought you could be the father."

"Your earlier messages were full of questions without coming right out and asking. Or conjecturing." He shook his head at the memory. "I glanced at a few, but after I looked you up online, I figured you were just digging for an inside track on the Texas Cattleman's Club for one of your stories."

That stung.

"And ignored me accordingly." She felt a self-deprecating smile twitch her lips. "I see you subscribe to the view that reporters are vultures."

"What was I supposed to think? It sure as hell

never crossed my mind you were writing to tell me I was—that I *might* be—a father." He shoved to his feet. "I should go. See the child for myself. Find out how to get tested."

She rose as well, feeling more off-kilter than she should have now that a potential daddy candidate for baby Micah was in town and seemed ready to take responsibility for the boy. The possible end of her involvement with the drama made her anxious. "Wait." She scrambled to stand, shoving her feet back into her worn slippers. "You can get DNA tests at Royal Memorial, although to expedite them is extremely expensive. But first, I should go with you to see Micah."

Colt studied her with those serious blue eyes. She felt weighed and measured, somehow, as if he were sizing up every last thing he knew about her. As a reporter, she should be used to the scrutiny. Instead, she felt suddenly aware that she wore only a thin pair of pajama pants and a sleep shirt.

"I'm definitely paying for the expedited tests. I'll stop by the hospital after I see Micah. And while it's generous of you to offer to go with me, Sierra, I can't ask you to do any more." He had a clipped way of speaking, articulating each word clearly. She wondered if it came from his time abroad. "I'm already deeply in your debt no matter how you view it."

"I haven't even told Cammie I was contacting

you," she hedged, feeling in her bones that she needed to be a part of the meeting. To see Micah's journey through to the end. "And we should let Micah's aunt, Eve, know that you're in town, too." There were so many people in Royal who'd rallied around Micah these last few months, people who'd helped piece together the mystery baby's story. "But if you want to meet Micah today, I'd prefer to be there with you. Cammie and Micah are staying with her fiancé, Drake Rhodes, a local rancher who has a house in town."

While he seemed to weigh this, she found herself wondering how he would do with the transition to caring for a six-month-old if he proved to be the father. Would it bring him any happiness, or only worry? Anxiety for Micah stirred again, her concern for the baby very real whether or not it made sense.

Finally, Colt nodded. "In that case, thank you."

"Great." She hurried toward the house. "It'll take me ten minutes to change and call Cammie. I'll fill her in and let her know we're coming. Then we'll go. I can drive."

She was halfway through the kitchen when Colt's voice behind her made her pause.

"Sierra. Can I ask you one more thing?"

She glanced back at him as he stood silhouetted in the doorway, his broad shoulders filling the entryway.

"Sure. Shoot." Leaning a hip on the stove, she tried to picture him cradling a baby. The answering image that splashed across her mind made her mourn her missing ovaries.

Reminding her sharply why she'd avoided relationships.

"Does he look like me at all?" Colt asked in that intense way of his, blue eyes boring right through her.

With that one simple question, she was toast. It was all she could do not to clutch her midsection where her reproductive organs should have been, her every maternal instinct touched.

And yet tormented.

She had to swallow back a hurt she hadn't allowed herself to indulge in years to consider the question.

"Actually, I think he does," she answered softly before spinning away. She beat a swift retreat to her room upstairs to regroup.

Get a grip.

Because she needed to keep an eye on Colt Black until she could be certain he was Micah's father. And even then, who was to say Colt could take good care of a baby? She would stick like glue to him through the transition until she knew for sure.

Two

In the passenger seat of Sierra's compact car, Colt couldn't stretch his legs in any way that didn't jam his knees into the glove box. Still, he appreciated the ride to Drake and Cammie's home in town where Micah was being fostered. More importantly, Colt was grateful for the escort Sierra provided now that it had become clear to him she'd played an integral role in the search for Micah's father.

Having Sierra at his side would speed things along at the Rhodes' home, assuring him the audience he needed. If Micah's aunt had trusted Sierra to use Arielle's diary to discreetly look into the identity of the baby's father, clearly Eve Martin had faith in her.

After the call to Cammie, Sierra said she called Eve Martin and updated her about Colt, his arrival in the U.S., and his desire to have a DNA test. Eve wasn't in town today, but she would meet with him tomorrow to discuss the situation. Clearly Micah's aunt was invested in her nephew's life.

"Have you met Cammie before? Or Drake Rhodes?" Sierra asked over the blaring radio as they headed into a more residential section of town.

Colt set aside his phone as Sierra turned down the music, a country pop song that had been loud enough to rattle the speakers. She hadn't even seemed to notice the noise until she'd spoken.

"I don't recall meeting either of them, but I've had business with Cammie's father before." He hadn't much cared for Tobias Wentworth five years ago when Colt had visited his ranch about a horse he'd been interested in purchasing. But according to local gossips, the guy's disposition had improved after his last marriage. "I hope Cammie is good with kids?"

He resented having to ask the question since it only reminded him that he hadn't done his duty toward Arielle. That he may have failed his own flesh and blood, too. The thought was all the more devastating considering how much emphasis his own beloved grandfather had placed on family. Colt had spent the last year trying to honor his relative's legacy by making the Royal Black Winery a success.

But what did that effort matter if Colt had over-looked his own son in the process?

"She's excellent with Micah," Sierra assured him, dragging her fingers through the blond strands that had escaped out a crack in the driver's side window. "I could see that on the very first day when she found him. I was first on the scene in the Royal Memorial Hospital parking lot after Cammie found him, you know. Cammie was totally smitten with the baby."

Would he be?

Colt's head throbbed at the reminder he had no idea what to do with an infant. He would need assistance. A nanny. But then again, he wouldn't allow himself to be the kind of father who delegated parenting.

After losing both parents in a small plane crash in early childhood, Colt had been raised by his grandfather. And while his granddad had been everything to him, Colt understood better than most people the way a kid craved family. Colt's life had been shaped by his parents' absence.

"Does she have help?" he wondered aloud, recognizing she must have adjusted her life a great deal to accommodate a new baby.

"Yes, that's part of the reason she moved in with Drake, so he could help out. Drake's stepsister is living there, and he has a housekeeper who watches

Micah sometimes. Plus Eve and I visit often and babysit if they need time away."

Colt didn't miss the wistful note in her voice. And this time, instead of feeling suspicious about the reporter's motives, he tucked away the observation for the future. If he couldn't find a nanny in a timely fashion, perhaps Sierra would consider lending a hand temporarily.

His attention wandered back to her again as she drove, her fingers drumming on the steering wheel while she navigated through Royal as easily as if she were a native. She'd changed into black jeans and boots, a soft gray sweater falling loosely off of one shoulder. She was pretty—not that he was in the market—but he would be a fool not to notice, and he wasn't a fool. He wanted to ask her about herself—only as a distraction—but a moment later she turned off the main road.

"Here we are." She pulled into a parking space outside a gracious two-story with a wide porch. She tugged her sunglasses from her nose before switching off the ignition. "Are you ready for this? You've been quiet."

"No stories today, right?" He needed to confirm this before moving forward. He remembered the reporters surrounding his house after his parents died, the media interest adding to the pain of an already harrowing time. "You said you wouldn't write anything else without the father's permission, but I'm well aware all of Royal wants to know who the father is. Gossip—even a whisper of information—travels fast."

He knew sooner or later he'd be tried in the court of public opinion, whether or not Sierra Morgan outed him in print. But today was too important to him, too personal, for him to worry about how a journalist would depict the moment.

"It's the *Royal Gazette*, not *TMZ*," she retorted as she shut off the engine. "And either way, I won't write anything about you and Micah unless you prove to be his father *and* you invite me to interview you."

Perhaps he shouldn't believe her. But as her green eyes met his—her expression restless and impatient—he found himself going with his gut and believing her anyway. Besides, he was too keyed up about the possibility of coming face-to-face with his maybe-son to worry about it any longer.

"Thank you." He gave a stiff nod before stepping from the cramped vehicle.

Sierra didn't wait for him. She was already out of the car and halfway up the flagstone walkway, clearly at ease here. But then, she said she visited often.

Was it strange to form that kind of bond with a baby simply because she'd been on site when he'd been found? Swallowing down his trepidation and uncertainty, he dragged his attention from Sierra's feminine form, her hair swaying in the mild spring breeze behind her. Instead, Colt focused on his next steps.

Meeting the boy who could be his son.

Certain she had to be imagining the weight of Colt's gaze on her as she walked, Sierra climbed the three wide steps up to the house. She had messaged Cammie to warn her they were on their way. Still, she knew how hard it had to be for her friend to open the door to a man who might be Micah's father.

As much as Cammie wanted Micah to have a family, Sierra strongly suspected the other woman would have been only too glad to take in the baby permanently. Her stomach knotted over the thought of a potential tug-of-war—even one of emotions, if not literally.

Now, Sierra rang the bell and waited, very aware of Colt's warm presence behind her. He wasn't standing close to her, yet she felt acutely attuned to him. The hint of spice she occasionally breathed in that she knew belonged to him. The muted rasp of silk over cotton from the lining of his jacket against his button-down as he shifted positions. The warmth he emanated.

The door pulled open before her thoughts carried her any farther down that precipitous path.

Cammie Wentworth, with her tall, elegant figure

and long red waves, stood framed in the doorway. "Hello, Sierra." Her green eyes turned to Colt. "I'm Cammie Wentworth."

Taking her hand, Colt nodded. "Colt Black. Thank you so much for seeing us on short notice."

"Certainly." Cammie's smile was all cool politeness as she studied Colt. "If Sierra says there's a good chance you're Micah's father, then it only made sense to meet as soon as possible. Her investigative skills rival local law enforcement." She opened the door wider and stepped back to admit them. "Please come in."

Moments later, they were seated in the comfortable great room decorated in blues and grays, a painting of dramatic basalt columns in coastal Australia dominating the space. A nod to Drake's time abroad.

Sierra wanted to offer to retrieve the baby—partly because she loved any excuse to hold Micah, but also because she was eager to see if the boy truly did resemble Colt the way she thought he did. But she wasn't Micah's guardian, and this wasn't her home, so she tried to wait patiently while Cammie asked Colt some of the questions that Sierra had already discussed with him—where he'd been, why he hadn't been in the baby's life before now and how he'd met Arielle.

Sierra's eyes were on the hallway that led to

Micah's room when she realized Colt was saying something she hadn't heard before.

"—we met after Arielle contacted me to ask for a meeting about some land I own on the outskirts of Royal. The old Fenwick land—"

"Violetta Ford's ranch," Sierra inserted quickly, wondering how much Colt knew about the local spinster rebel who'd posed as a man—Vincent Fenwick—so she could claim a place in the Texas Cattleman's Club.

The story was one of many gems she'd uncovered about the history of the club, and one of the most compelling reasons to write a book about that saga.

"You know about that?" Colt turned to her from his seat on a leather ottoman, surprise in his blue eyes. "Arielle told me the tale that night—the only night we were together. I wasn't aware of that story. I'd just bought the land as an investment."

Sierra's reporter brain clicked into high gear, wondering how she could gain access to that land. Emmalou Hillard, the ninety-nine-year-old Royal resident who'd once been a cowgirl on Violetta Ford's ranch had told Sierra that Violetta kept a diary. And that she thought it was buried on the ranch. Sierra would love to get her hands on it for the sake of the book she wanted to write.

Cammie leaned forward, her silver pendant swinging with the movement as she addressed Colt.

"Did you know Sierra has taken up Arielle's work to uncover some of the TCC's lost past? Sierra already helped solve the mystery of Harmon Wentworth's birth mother."

Sierra smiled her thanks at Cammie, appreciating the way the other woman depicted her investigative efforts as helpful instead of intrusive. Sierra recalled plenty of times Cammie had tried to dodge her at first, convinced Sierra only wanted a scoop. But eventually, she'd won her over.

"That's kind of you, but Tate Wentworth was the one who finally put all the pieces together," she reminded Cammie. Sierra knew Cammie wasn't close with her second cousin, but the other woman surely knew that it was Tate who'd stolen pages from Arielle Martin's diary that led to the truth. Tate had then found out about Violetta Ford's long ago affair with Dean Wentworth, Harmon's father.

"But you weren't stopping until you had answers," Cammie shot back. "You lit a fire under all of us."

"Really?" Colt swiveled to look at Sierra. "I didn't even know Harmon was adopted."

Sierra folded her arms, uncomfortable with the spotlight on her. Especially when there was a new mystery to solve. One that tugged at Sierra's heart far more than Harmon's background.

"I haven't spent *all* my time in Royal hounding you," she admitted. "I'm collecting stories about the

Texas Cattleman's Club for a book. That's one of the reasons I took a leave of absence from *America* magazine. The other was finding Micah's father."

Both Colt and Cammie looked like they might say more about the subject, so Sierra sprang to her feet. She needed to keep the meeting on track. Focused on what was most important.

"Cammie, do you feel comfortable letting Colt meet Micah?" Her natural drive and bluntness had carried her far as a reporter.

It hadn't done her many favors socially.

But Cammie didn't seem to take offense. She nodded slowly. Solemnly. "I feel very comfortable. While I haven't met Colt before, I ran into his grandfather often at the Texas Cattleman's Club." She turned to Colt, and her expression softened. "I'm so sorry for your loss. Clyde Black was a good man."

"Thank you." Colt's throat worked on a swallow before he continued. "I appreciate that."

Cammie moved toward the hallway. "I'll get Micah."

Something about the gravity of her tone made Sierra remember how hard this would be on her friend if she had to give up Micah. Sierra's heart squeezed in empathy while Cammie disappeared down the hall.

Colt's voice called her from her thoughts. "You've

got better sleuthing skills than local law enforcement?"

She shrugged as she paced the great room to work off some of her nervous energy, unsure why she felt so keyed up.

"Investigative reporting involves far more research than actual writing," she explained, curious if he only asked to distract himself from the implications of the impending meeting with Micah. Was Colt nervous? "Most of my time is spent chasing down leads."

"And now you're writing a book." His blue eyes followed her as she circled the long sectional couch. "Will that keep you as busy as your last job?"

She guessed he was making small talk, and yet his attention—his interest— stirred something to life inside her that had been dormant for a long time. It had to be simple physical attraction, didn't it? She was just unaccustomed to the way a man's notice could heighten all the senses. Stuffing down the awareness, she tried to give the question consideration.

"I hope so." She would be the one in need of distraction once the mystery of baby Micah was solved. Cammie wouldn't be the only one with an empty space in her heart after the little boy departed from their lives. "I wouldn't have taken on the project if I didn't think there was a lot to uncover here."

Then again, Micah had been another reason that

she'd justified remaining in Royal long after the gala celebrating the tenth anniversary of women in the TCC. That may have been her impetus for coming to town, but she'd certainly been swept up in a bigger drama from day one.

She circled the room faster. Where was Cammie?

"And what do you think you'll be uncovering?" Colt came to his feet, stepping into her path before she passed the ottoman where he'd been sitting. "Secrets people would rather remain hidden? Scandals that will only hurt club members if they come to light?"

She drew back a step at the glittering accusation in his eyes. Also, the warmth of his nearness sent sensations skittering up her arms and over her shoulders. Down her back.

"So much for being forever in my debt for informing you about Micah," she muttered, cranking her neck to look up at him. "You're already convinced I'm going to do a hatchet job with the book and I haven't even started."

They stood too close to one another in wordless stand-off until Cammie's voice sounded from the entrance to the great room.

"Here he is, Colt. Meet Arielle's son, Micah."

For an instant, it felt like that moment on the playground as a kid when he'd fallen off the monkey bars and had the wind knocked out of him. Time stopped along with his breath, a frozen pause when he felt powerless to move. To think. To understand what was happening.

Logically, he could see Cammie Wentworth heading toward him with a dark-haired baby in her arms. The kid was a charmer, too, dark eyes wide and alert as he gripped the bare toes of one foot, a happy smile curving his lips as he seemed to bounce to unheard music. He wore a blue cotton one-piece outfit printed with dump trucks.

Was this even happening?

Colt still hadn't moved when Sierra laid a light hand on his arm.

"Oh, Colt, isn't he precious?" she murmured, her voice full of wonder. "He gets more adorable every time I see him, and I would have never thought that was possible."

Something about her fingers resting on his upper arm, a brief, feminine touch that glanced off him, nudged Colt back to life. She buzzed with so much restless energy all the time, maybe she'd shocked him out of the momentary stasis.

"May I hold him?" he asked, surprising himself.

He had no experience with kids, much less babies. But this was different.

Because he knew immediately this child belonged to him. With him. Except for the darker complexion of the child's skin and the deep brown of wide, curious eyes, the little boy could have been a mirror image of Colt's own babyhood.

And having been orphaned himself at an early age, he refused to let his son feel the painful loneliness that came with feeling abandoned. Colt had watched his grandfather step up to take on the parent role even though there was no way the old man had bargained for that much involvement in Colt's life. Now it was Colt's turn to step up. To fill a void where two parents should be and at least give the child one.

"Of course," Cammie agreed, stepping closer to make the exchange.

Sierra hovered close by, making soft cooing sounds at the infant, who rewarded her with a big, gummy smile, then kicked the foot he was holding.

"He's a wiggle worm." Sierra laughed delightedly at the boy's antics while Colt scooped him from Cammie's arms and into his own.

And if he'd thought the world had stopped when the baby arrived in the room, that incident was nothing compared to staring into the child's brown eyes for the first time.

"Hello, Micah," he said softly. Overcome as his world shifted.

Old priorities fell away as a new reality coalesced around this tiny life that he knew in his bones was his son. Micah C. was Micah Colt. No ifs, ands or buts about it.

Micah lifted one hand to his mouth, gently gnawing his fingers as he studied Colt.

He moved toward one of the large windows flanking the fireplace, wanting to study the baby's features more closely. Needing to memorize every line, every curve of the boy's face.

His. Son.

In his peripheral vision, Colt saw Sierra moved to one side of the room to speak quietly to Cammie. Discussing the possibility of his being Micah's father? Or letting Cammie know his plan to pay the fee for the expedited DNA test?

He'd called the hospital on the way here and learned that—for an exorbitant fee—results could be processed in twenty-four hours.

And as much as Colt wanted to spend more time with the tiny person in his arms, he knew he needed to get the wheels in motion to bring Micah home with him. Which meant the sooner he got to Royal Memorial Hospital, the sooner he could bring Micah home with him.

Where his son belonged.

"What do you think?" Sierra asked from just behind him, her fingers reaching around Micah to stroke a knuckle over the baby's round cheek.

Micah's eyes blinked heavily, as if the soft caress could put him to sleep.

"I think I need a ride to Royal Memorial," he in-

JOANNE ROCK 41

formed her, shifting his gaze from Micah's face to hers. "But I'm happy to call for a car."

The enrapt expression he spied on her face brought home how much Sierra cared about the boy. She'd admitted as much, but Colt hadn't really appreciated the full extent of her feelings until he saw that unguarded, tender look in her eyes.

There wasn't a doubt in his mind that she would be an attentive sitter for the child if Colt needed help in the coming weeks.

But if he invited her into their lives—however briefly—could he trust her not to sniff out secrets and scandals for her book while he tried to rebuild his life here?

"The hospital is on the route to the B and B," she reminded him, green eyes lifting to his, her hand still cradled against the baby's cheek. "I can drop you off there on my way home."

He nodded as he moved toward Cammie to return the boy to her safekeeping. "That would be great. And thank you, Cammie. I appreciate you letting me see him."

Cammie shifted the boy to her opposite shoulder, tucking him against her with the practiced ease of any mother. "You're going to get the DNA test?"

"I am." Filled with new purpose, Colt realized he had a lot to plan. Starting with a call to his housekeeper in France to pack some of his things since he wouldn't be returning to the winery for at least a month or two. It looked like he'd be in Royal for the local Wine and Roses Festival after all. "If the test turns out the way I think it will, I'll speak to Arielle's sister and the social worker about taking over parenting duties immediately. With any luck, I can return tomorrow afternoon."

"So soon?" Cammie asked, her gaze darting to Sierra and then back to him.

But the timetable was fixed.

"It's not soon enough from my perspective," he reminded the baby's foster parent, hoping she understood his need to establish an overdue relationship with the boy. "I can't thank you enough for taking such good care of Micah. I know I'll never get back the months I've already lost not knowing about him. So if the test proves I'm his father, I will be back as soon as possible to start a new life with my son."

Three

Pacing her room at the Cimarron Rose, Sierra wondered how many more laps it would take to wear a hole right through the braided rug. Surely not that many, given that she'd been practically sprinting circles around the small space while waiting for a text from Colt.

Or a phone call.

Heck, she would have settled for smoke signals at this point.

She just wanted to know what had happened with the DNA test.

Would Colt ignore her now that she'd pointed him in Micah's direction? Maybe in his eyes, she'd served her purpose in informing him about the baby, and now she was out of the picture. In theory, she understood that the results of the DNA test were his personal business. He had no obligation to inform her, even though she'd been totally invested in finding Micah's father from the moment she'd seen the baby carrier on the trunk of Cammie Wentworth's Mercedes that day in the Royal Memorial Hospital parking lot.

But damn it. She at least deserved to know if he *wasn't* the boy's father so she could continue her search. She braked to a halt in front of the window overlooking the tree and courtyard where she'd sat with Colt just the day before, navigating an awkward conversation about his relationship with Arielle. He'd filled her thoughts nearly every moment since then. Only because of his connection to Micah, she told herself. Not because Colt intrigued her with his caring eyes and broad shoulders. Gently, Sierra pounded her fist on the wooden sill, willing her phone to ring. For Colt to give her answers.

More than twenty-four hours had passed since she'd dropped Colt in front of the hospital doors the day before.

Surely he'd heard something about the DNA test results by now?

Abandoning her short-lived attempt to be patient, Sierra resumed her pacing. She lifted her phone to look at the messages she'd sent to Colt over the past week, scanning the notes until she came to the most recent one that had finally spurred him to get on a plane.

Please respond, it began, before dropping the bombshell baby news. Of course, he hadn't responded. At least not by text. She'd been stunned to see him at her door a day later and hadn't thought to make sure he let her know his next step.

Now her thumbs got to work.

Could you let me know what you learn about a potential family connection to Micah either way? I want to be sure I find his father, and if it's not you, I must return to the drawing board.

Rereading it, she hit Send before she could second-guess the wording. With a sigh, she tossed the device onto the middle of the four-poster bed, where it landed with a soft plunk.

Would Colt answer? He couldn't possibly understand how much the search for Micah's dad meant to her after growing up without knowing the identity of her own birth parents. But Sierra recognized the trail would go cold if she didn't press for answers now. That's what had happened to her as an abandoned infant. Her adoptive parents hadn't started a search in earnest until Sierra turned twelve, after she convinced them that it was important to her. Twelve years had been too long.

Beep. Beep.

The electronic chime of her phone made the mattress vibrate underneath the device.

Sierra dove on it, snatching up the cell. The notification was for a call, not a text. And, to her surprise, Colt's name displayed across the top of her screen. Stabbing the button, she answered as quickly as possible.

"Colt? How did it go?" She hadn't realized until this moment how worried she was that the baby might *not* be his. Would he be disappointed? Relieved?

Her stomach knotted at either scenario.

"The DNA is a match," he said quietly, his tone unreadable.

Her throat went tight with tension, her gut churning. A thousand reactions spun through her. Was he calling solely as a courtesy? Would he allow her to see Micah anymore? How did Cammie and Eve take the news? She sank to the edge of the mattress, knowing she needed to proceed carefully with Colt if she wanted to continue to spend time with the precious baby she'd grown to care for deeply.

And she did. Her heart couldn't bear the thought of being shut out of Micah's life.

"You knew it would be," she reminded him, thinking how confident he'd seemed the day before when they left Drake's house. "Congratulations, Colt. Micah is lucky to have you for a father."

She'd seen the determination to be a good father in his eyes when he'd looked at Micah. Still, the fast shift in Colt's life had to leave his head spinning.

"Thank you," he replied, his voice still unnaturally low. "Although I'm not sure Micah would agree with you. He cried the whole way from Cammie's house to the ranch."

Her heart clutched to envision baby tears.

"Aw. How hard for you both. Babies cry though, Colt, and Micah is going through a big change right now." She tried to reassure him, even as she yearned to check on Micah for herself. See with her own eyes that the sweet little boy was okay. "Is he better now?"

"He fell asleep moments ago," Colt explained, the cause of his near whisper immediately becoming clear. "And even though Cammie and Eve gave me four pages of schedules and instructions to ensure I do the right things, I'm man enough to admit I'm staring at the crib in pure terror for the moment he wakes up again."

A smile tugged at her lips to imagine the big, strong rancher at the utter mercy of his infant son.

"I'd love to see him if you'd like some moral support for your first day of fatherhood." She would like to think she only offered in order to assure herself Micah was in good hands. That Colt had all he needed to care for the little boy.

But she couldn't deny that Colt had been in her

thoughts ever since she'd dropped him off at the hospital. He'd stirred something inside her.

There was a spark between them.

"You'd do that?" He sounded more suspicious than grateful.

Raising every one of Sierra's hackles. Spark or no spark, that frustrated her.

"Why does that seem so hard to believe? Just because I'm a journalist doesn't mean I'm immune to the universal appeal of babies. Even reporters have hearts, you know. And maternal instincts." She realized she'd snapped too hard as soon as the last bit tumbled out of her mouth.

But then, she was mighty defensive of her inability to have babies. Not that Colt had any way of knowing.

"You're right," he acknowledged, then let out a gusty sigh. "I guess I'm so preoccupied about what to do next with a baby, it's hard for me to remember that not everyone views this as scary."

Sierra stared at her toes resting on the bright braided rug in her room at the B and B, waiting for Colt's verdict on if he wanted her there or not. Her gaze went to the antique globe on the oak desk, where the side of the world with France was visible from her search to find the man on the other end of the phone.

Was it any wonder he was overwhelmed by parenting when just three days ago he was walking among his grapevines in his small town north of Toulouse, completely oblivious that he'd fathered a son on the other side of the world?

"Are you still there?" he asked when she—uncharacteristically—hadn't rushed to fill the silence.

"I am. But I won't plead my case when I've already offered help. I can't make you trust me." She understood that, even as it ruffled her feathers.

With an idle finger, she spun the globe, shoving away the sight of Colt's other home.

"It's not a matter of trust."

"No? Because I've been in Royal for five months, earning other people's faith in me. But you don't know me. I get it." She'd had an uphill battle from the first day she'd arrived in Royal. With Cammie. With the cop, Haley Lopez, who'd responded to the call about an abandoned child. With Harmon Wentworth, who hadn't known who his biological mother was. Arielle Martin had started the search, and Sierra got the conclusion for Harmon.

Sierra had liked to think she'd helped them all in some small way or another. Yet as far as Colt was concerned, she was just another journalist pariah digging for dirt on other people.

"Sierra, you told me you weren't writing a story, and I believe you." He sounded sincere.

"Then what's keeping you from accepting my help when you know Micah is unsettled from the change?" she pushed, exasperated. "Clearly you're feeling out of your element today. Imagine how Micah feels?"

"I am out of my element." He paused. "But I'm also attracted to you."

The surprise admission bowled her over. She gripped the corner of the duvet like a lifeline, waiting to feel steady again.

"Oh. I—" She reached for words but found she didn't have any. Because even though she'd felt the spark between them, too, she'd never imagined Colt would confront it head-on.

"That makes the time we spend together more problematic. But I can assure you that I won't act on it." The grim determination in his voice was hardly flattering, but she understood his reticence.

Respected it even, considering all that he had on his plate right now. Although a little part of her might have felt disappointed, too. Which made no sense when she was committed to avoiding romantic entanglements. She didn't need relationships in her life that would only necessitate telling someone else why she couldn't have children.

"Okay then," she continued carefully, her senses all attuned to his every breath and nuance of sound over the phone. "I understand. And my offer still stands."

She could hear the relief in the long breath he let out.

"Thank you so much, Sierra. Micah and I are

staying at the old Fenwick ranch house. I'd be grateful for help anytime you can make it over here."

She hadn't forgotten about his connection to the Fenwick house. At the mention of it now, Sierra's brain started running in high speed again. That's where Violetta's diary was rumored to be hidden. Not that she would go searching for it today when Colt needed her help with Micah. And she hated the idea that looking for the diary would somehow confirm Colt's worst opinions about her. But she would figure out how to deal with it later. She wouldn't turn down this chance to spend time with Micah. Reassure the baby with her presence.

"I'll be there within the hour," she promised, hurrying to her closet to find something to wear besides pajama pants.

And yes, call her contrary, but she searched for something both feminine and pretty.

Even if they weren't *acting* on the mutual attraction, she couldn't pretend it didn't exist. Being around Colt made her feel hyperaware, all her senses heightened. It had been four years since she'd ended her last relationship to focus on her career. To ignore the conflicted feelings she had about her body and motherhood. Four long years without a romantic relationship hadn't seemed like a chore at that time, but right now, with the promise of spending time with Colt looming, she felt every one of those years without a man's touch.

As long as she continued to ignore the sparks between them, she'd be okay. Because if she wanted an invitation to the Fenwick house in the future to search for the diary, she needed to maintain a good relationship with Colt Black.

Staring down into his son's portable crib in the middle of the living room floor, Colt let the magnitude of the moment wash over him.

He stood alone in the rambling old Fenwick ranch house with his *son*.

How many times would he have to think it and say it in order for the news to sink in? The idea that he had fathered a child still felt surreal, as did this entire trip to Royal.

His hand flexed on one padded bar of the portacrib as he wondered what his grandfather would say if Clyde Black could see Colt now. Colt had briefly considered bringing Micah to the house Colt had grown up in before dismissing the idea. The home at Black Ranch still felt too empty without his grandfather's presence, even though it had been over a year since Granddad's death. The Fenwick place was smaller, but Colt had hired a crew to oversee renovation work while he'd been abroad. Now, most of the indoor changes were complete with a renovated kitchen, living areas and three bedrooms. There was an in-law suite that still needed work, and some exterior updates. But Colt appreciated that the space felt scrubbed clean, like a fresh start for him and Micah.

A soft tapping at the front of the house called his attention from his musing.

Shoving to his feet from the end of a chaise lounge, Colt strode to the front door. He caught a glimpse of Sierra's petite figure through one of the sidelights, and his anticipation ratcheted up a few notches. Which was all wrong, damn it.

He hadn't come to terms with the hurt he'd brought to Arielle's and Micah's lives by not checking in with her after their night together. So he had no business feeling an attraction to Sierra now, when the thought of Arielle pregnant and alone still haunted him.

Steeling himself against the inevitable tug of desire he was powerless to halt, Colt opened the door.

Sierra stood on the deep porch in a denim skirt and boots, the sheer hem of a turquoise-colored beaded blouse blowing in the spring breeze as she smiled up at him. She clutched a reusable shopping bag in one arm, a baguette peeking out of the top.

"I'm so glad you heard me knocking. I didn't want to ring the bell if Micah was still napping, and even tapping at the door felt risky." Her green gaze darted past him to peer into the house. "Is he still asleep?"

A long, piercing wail answered the question.

Colt's chest ached at the sound, but before he

could formulate a response, Sierra was stepping inside the house.

"May I go to him?" she asked, settling the grocery sack on a plank table in the foyer, her eyes already on the portable crib in the living room.

"Sure. I'd be grateful. And I'm certain he'll be glad to see a familiar face." He stepped out of her way, feeling helpless. "I need a crash course in infant care," he explained, wondering if there was such a thing. "I have Cammie on speed dial, but if I spend some time watching you with him, I'll have a better feel for how to respond tomorrow."

Colt doubted if she heard a single word he said, however. As soon as he'd given her the green light, she dashed past him in a blur of turquoise, cooing soft sounds of empathy for Micah's unhappiness. Colt closed the door behind her and followed her inside.

"My goodness, so much sadness," she prattled softly to the boy, plucking him from the crib to hold him against her shoulder. "It's all okay," she soothed, rubbing a hand along his back. "You're going to love your new house with your daddy."

Daddy.

Another word to send Colt reeling.

He met his son's gaze in time to see a tear roll down the chubby cheek. The child had stopped making any sounds though, perhaps startled into silence to listen to Sierra, the baby whisperer.

Unable to resist the urge to wipe away the boy's tear, Colt smoothed a knuckle under one brown eye while Micah arched back in an attempt to see Sierra's face. Using his arms to push at her shoulder, Micah's fingers wound into her hair until he clutched a handful of her flaxen-colored hair.

"Is he hurting you?" Colt asked, steadying the tiny fist, and wondering if he should try to pry it open and free her hair.

Sierra glanced up at him over her shoulder, their three heads all close together. He'd never been this near her, in fact. And he became aware of several things at once.

Her hair was silky soft. Strands tickled over the back of his hand as he tried to prevent Micah from pulling any, and the feel of it made him long to spear his own fingers through the long mass.

Then there was her scent. She smelled like orange blossoms, a fragrance that suited her perfectly—sweet with a zing that tingled in his nose.

Finally, he noticed that Sierra's lips were soft and full, a shade of deep, rosy red that made him ache for a taste.

It would have been difficult enough if he'd been cataloging all those things about her on his own. But she didn't look away from him either. Almost as if she were as compelled by this pull between them as he felt.

"Um." She made a small hum of sound that went

right through him. "I should probably change him. Where—"

"I know how to do that much," Colt assured her, grateful to her for breaking the moment with something so practical. "I had Cammie show me before I left her house. She and Eve Martin gave me a rundown of the basics before they gave the green light for me to take him." Reaching for Micah, he tried to be careful not to touch Sierra.

Much.

"I don't mind—" she began, her breath hitching as his forearm grazed her breast.

Colt ground his teeth against the heat that sizzled through him from the feel of her.

"I've got it. Diapers are upstairs," he explained too brusquely, heading for the staircase with quick, determined steps.

She might have said something about the groceries, or dinner, but Colt was too busy making his abrupt exit to answer.

He should be focused on his son, after all. Not the unexpectedly appealing reporter who'd united him with Micah. Or how soft she would feel against him.

"Don't worry, big guy," he said to Micah, who gnawed on his forefinger while staring at Colt. "We're going to get through this, I promise."

Did the baby recognize Colt's lack of training?

As they entered the room Colt had designated as

a nursery, Micah's brown gaze appeared thoughtful. Questioning. As if he wondered why Colt had intercepted him from the arms of the sweetly scented, tender woman who'd held him earlier.

"She's only temporary, buddy," he informed the boy as he laid him on the changing table. Colt had spent the night before shopping online for the most important pieces of baby furniture. The cherrywood nursery set and other baby equipment had been delivered that morning. "So don't get too attached."

Micah frowned, slapping the thick white changing pad with one hand as if to protest the news while Colt passed him a rattle and got to work on the task at hand.

"I hear you. And I empathize," he assured him. "I'm not in any hurry for her to leave either."

And not because he was attracted to her. Far from it. Asking her to help temporarily with Micah would be easier if he didn't feel this pull toward her every time they were in the same room.

But Micah deserved a familiar face around while he got used to Colt, didn't he? That was the least Colt could do for his son after the way he'd failed the boy by not being with him from the beginning.

"Ba-boo," Micah announced, his brown eyes still serious while Colt finished cleaning him up. "Ba-boo!" he said again, more urgently.

Colt knew a six-month-old wasn't really giving him advice. But the child's face was so serious.

Like mine.

How many times had people told Colt he was too serious? His grandfather for one, and Clyde Black had been one of the few people in the world whose opinion mattered to Colt.

The connection gave Colt a pang as he taped the clean diaper into place and tugged a fresh white onesie covered with elephants over Micah's wiggly limbs.

Colt couldn't deny that he'd always taken a practical, methodical approach to life.

Son, you need to live a little. Find what brings you joy.

He could hear Granddad's voice in his head even now. That advice had driven Colt to move to France to fulfill his grandfather's dream of owning a winery. And while he took pride and satisfaction in that accomplishment, it hadn't necessarily brought Colt *joy* since it hadn't been *his* dream.

What if Micah was already genetically predisposed to be as solemn as his father? The idea troubled Colt in a way the characteristic had never bothered him in himself.

From the doorway came a sudden squeaky sound, making both Micah and Colt turn to see a blue stuffed bunny rabbit with tall, fluffy ears. Slowly, the bunny lowered to reveal Sierra's face, making Micah giggle.

Had there ever been a sound so sweet?

As baby laughter filled the room, Colt acknowledged that—while Sierra Morgan might have a serious side—she sure knew how to turn that off around Micah. She was fun, playful and kind. Exactly the right personality to help Micah transition into his new home.

The fact that she was also smart, thoughtful and sexy as hell shouldn't matter.

"How did it go?" Sierra asked as she walked deeper into the room, passing the stuffed bunny to Micah. "He sounds happy."

Colt's eyes wandered over her even as he wondered how he would handle having her around more often if he was fortunate enough to talk her into helping him with Micah.

"That had more to do with you than me," Colt acknowledged, lifting Micah in his arms, cradling the precious weight against his chest. "Which is why I'm hoping you'll consider a more formal arrangement for spending some time with him as he transitions into living with me."

Her pale eyebrows scrunched together. "What kind of arrangement?"

"I know you're working on a book about the Texas Cattleman's Club. But I wondered if, temporarily, you might be persuaded to work on it from here. While spending more time with Micah." The boy wriggled, and Colt tried to shift his hold on him, but Sierra lifted him into her arms.

Bringing her scent and softness enticingly close for a moment. Scrambling his thoughts.

"Like a nanny?" She shook her head even as she said the word. "I'm happy to babysit anytime, Colt. I did that to help out Cammie, too. He knows me, so that would keep him from having to get used to another stranger."

He winced at the idea of himself as a stranger. But he had to acknowledge it was true. He was a stranger to his own son.

"I need far more help than Cammie. At least for the next couple of weeks." Extending his arms, he gestured to the house around them. "I'm still trying to set up the house to be sure it's babyproof. And you can see I have a lot to learn about caring for an infant."

"You're doing really well, especially for being tossed into parenthood with so little time to prepare," she interjected, moving around the room to keep Micah engaged, showing him the mobile over the bassinet one moment, and then moving to look out the upstairs window with him the next.

"You'd be well-compensated, of course," he pressed, recognizing that he didn't need just anyone to help with Micah. He wanted *her*. She was good with his son. Micah already knew her. And her playful spirit would make this difficult transition easier for the more reserved Black males. "And there are plenty of rooms here. The Fenwick house is a historic Royal property."

Sierra's head swiveled toward him. "You want me to move in?"

Something about the way she said it sent awareness tripping up his spine. Briefly, he recalled his reservations about getting close to her because of her work. But the truth would come out about his parentage of Micah either way. He had nothing to hide.

"At least for a couple of weeks. A month, perhaps." He hoped he wasn't imposing. But as he stared at her slender arms wrapped around his son, her pretty face deep in thought even as Micah tugged on a few strands of her hair, Colt was prepared to meet any demand to keep her here. Micah needed her with him. "Just until I find a rhythm with caregiving, and then you can help me carefully vet a nanny."

When her green eyes met his, there was a hint of conflict in them. Reservation.

"You said it yourself, Sierra," he pressed, reminding her of what she'd told him about the unfamiliar surroundings for a baby. "Micah knows you. It will help him if you're around while we make this transition."

Her expression softened. Whatever concerns she'd had about the arrangement privately, she seemed to have set them aside at the idea of the baby needing her.

"In that case, Colt, how can I say no?" A smile lifted one side of her full lips.

Relieved to have secured her help with his son, Colt tucked away his own reservations. Though briefly he wondered if they mirrored whatever Sierra's concerns had been.

One way or another, they'd avoid the attraction for the sake of the child.

Yet as he followed Sierra out of the nursery into the dim lights of the hall, where his gaze was drawn to the sway of her curved hips, Colt recognized the next month together wouldn't be easy.

Four

Was there a better scent than a freshly bathed baby?

After dressing Micah, Sierra breathed in the fragrant baby shampoo as she kissed the top of his still-damp head where dark hair already curled after a splash-filled bath time. Colt had helped her with the chore to ready his son for bed, and they'd both ended up wet.

Which was how she'd ended up wearing one of Colt's T-shirts, the soft cotton containing her other favorite new scent—the pine and sandalwood notes of Colt.

Her temporary housemate.

Sierra had accepted the dry shirt, although Colt

had bolted right afterward, insisting he should finish making their dinner. No doubt he'd been feeling the full impact of complicated awareness, too.
She could hardly beg off the meal now since she'd
been the one to bring over fresh bread and a few
groceries, just in case he needed a hand with dinner. When she'd first arrived, she'd assumed she'd
have to talk Colt into letting her see Micah again.

She'd been unprepared for his offer—no, his
urging—for her to take on a nanny role for the
next few weeks. The idea thrilled her, of course, because she already loved Colt's son. But it made her
realize how difficult it would be to separate from
the boy once Colt found a replacement caregiver.

By then, she'd be that much more attached to
Micah.

As if that wasn't complicated enough, there was
the matter of an attraction that Colt had freely admitted to her. An attraction strong enough to have
him bolting from the bathroom after they'd shared
laughter, bumping elbows, and wet clothes.

Sierra hugged Micah closer at the memory, hoping the baby would distract her from the unfamiliar
ache for Colt's touch. If only Micah would be there
with them all evening to act as the perfect baby barrier. But Colt had specifically timed this meal for
after they put Micah to bed.

Which meant she was already twitchy with the

thought of so much alone time with Micah's hot daddy.

"We'd better go check on him," she told Micah, nuzzling against his temple in a way that made the boy giggle a little. He was already sleepy, his hold on the stuffed bunny she'd brought for him getting looser.

Leaving the nursery that Colt had apparently outfitted overnight, Sierra carried Micah through the rambling old farmhouse and down the stairs toward the kitchen. The Fenwick ranch had been renovated in the last months. The paint colors—muted blues and yellows—made for inviting rooms. The open floor plan downstairs had to have been reimagined, since that certainly hadn't been the architectural preference when Violetta Ford had the house built. Sierra tried to imagine where the walls had once been, yet couldn't envision the layout any other way.

Now, a fire had been laid in the hearth that flanked the dining area, where a sturdy farmhouse table had been set with simple white dishes. Two pink azalea branches in a bud vase served as a centerpiece, while in the kitchen beyond, Colt slid a ladle into a red stoneware pot.

When had a man last cooked for her? A long ago boyfriend had warmed up soup from a can once when she'd had a cold. At the time, she'd been touched. But that experience hadn't come close to the way it made her feel to see Colt's efforts for her now.

Efforts he made only because he was grateful she'd agreed to help him with Micah, she reminded herself. There wasn't anything remotely romantic about it. It was just an exceptionally nice thank-you.

"Whatever you're making smells amazing." She breathed in the aromatic scents, trying to identify the meal.

Colt laid a towel over his shoulder and shut off the burner under the pot still on the stove. "Coq au vin is one of the few French dishes I learned to make while I lived overseas, but I figured with that in my cooking repertoire, how much else do I need?"

Turning toward her, he held out his hands to take Micah.

Sierra moved closer to pass the baby, their arms brushing. Awareness hummed through her, even as she tried to focus on Colt's words and not his touch.

"It sounds impressive, but I will confess I know nothing about cooking beyond hitting the microwave button for the time listed on the back of a frozen meal." Back in Houston, she'd purposely distanced herself from all things domestic, convinced she could be happy making her work the focal point of her life.

Colt chuckled as he stepped back, securing Micah easily in one arm.

"I'm suddenly feeling all the more confident in my cooking prowess." His blue eyes met hers as they stood under one of the industrial pendant lamps. "But is it time to eat yet? Should we lay him in his crib first? Cammie gave me a schedule. I can check."

"It's okay. We've got this. We might as well try. I brought him down so we could put him to bed together." Her gaze moved to Micah as the boy laid his head on Colt's shoulder, as if he were too tired to hold it up any longer. With their faces so close to one another, Sierra could see the resemblance all the more. The shape of the eyes. The hairline around their temples. "Aw, look at him. He looks like he could doze off any minute."

"What do you think, big guy?" Colt asked, laying his cheek against his son's head. "Want to give the new crib a test run?"

Micah squeezed the ear of his bunny and gave the animal a shake, his eyelids drooping.

Sierra's heart turned over to see the two of them look comfortable together for the moment. "That looks like a yes to me."

Together, they ascended the stairs to the nursery. Sierra tried not to think about the intimacy of the act. And her gaze definitely didn't search the hallway for the door that might lead to Colt's room. She still couldn't believe she was going to move in with him for a few weeks. A tingle shot through her at the thought of more nights together like this.

"Are you sure he's okay in a room by himself?" Colt asked as they entered the nursery. "I read conflicting things online."

The room had been painted a mellow shade of blue. Pale gray curtains and wall art depicting line drawings of the Fenwick ranch gave the room a more adult appeal, but the cherrywood furniture and abundant toys showed that Colt had tried his best to make it kid-friendly in the last twenty-four hours.

"Cammie just transitioned him to his own room, so I think he'll be fine. But if he's too fretful, we can move him to the portable crib, and he can sleep with one of us." The thought of inviting herself over for the night made her cheeks warm. "I mean, not that I'm spending tonight here. But other nights, he can sleep in my room if that works best."

If he noticed that she was flustered, she couldn't tell. His expression had turned serious again.

"The sooner you can move in the better, as far as I'm concerned, but I understand you might not be ready to stay with us tonight."

Sierra's mouth went dry at the thought of time spent under the same roof as this magnetic man who wanted to cook for her and who respected what she had to offer as a caregiver to a child. All the years that she'd been ignoring the lure of domestic comforts came back to bite her now.

"Let's see how he's doing once we've finished our dinner, and we can decide from there," she suggested, needing to make this night about Micah and not about the waves of awareness rolling over her.

Threatening to pull her under a tide of longing.

"Sounds like a plan." Colt turned from her to face the crib. "Now, how do I go about putting him down? Is there rocking involved?"

"If he needed soothing, I would say yes to the rocking. But he looks content to me, so maybe just lay him down gently on his back and see what happens?" She was no expert. But she'd read a lot before babysitting Micah in an effort to make sure she gleaned as much as possible about caring for an infant. "And the bunny can't go in the crib with him."

She took the stuffed toy from Micah's hand and set it aside.

Colt shifted his son closer to the crib before turning to her again. "Should we dim the lights? Wind the mobile?"

"I'm on it." She couldn't quite stifle a smile at the thought he put into the bedtime routine.

Then again, if she'd been able to have children, she probably would have been the same way. A tightness knotted in her chest as she reached over the crib to wind a mobile of brightly colored horses. By the time the device started playing a comforting lullaby tune, Sierra was already halfway across the room to turn down the overhead lights.

"There you go, buddy," Colt told him. With a kiss on the baby's forehead, he leaned broad shoulders over the crib and lowered the boy onto the thick mattress. "Sleep well."

Sierra's heart melted a little to watch them together. She dialed down the brightness on the switch, casting the nursery in a soft glow. Making the room feel more intimate.

Her nerves pinged with awareness.

"Do you have the baby monitor set up?" she asked, reminding herself to get used to this.

But sharing a bedtime routine with a decidedly hot rancher was going to test her commitment to avoiding romantic entanglements. Especially when getting entangled with Colt Black had a definite appeal.

"I do." Colt frowned down at Micah, who seemed content to kick his foot, his diaper crinkling under his onesie with every move. "I read that no one uses a blanket on infants anymore, but it seems strange to lay him down without one."

She was grateful for Colt's focus on his son, which kept him from reading the runaway thoughts in her expression. Bracing herself to get closer to him again, she kept her attention on the crib as she returned to his side.

"I know, right?" Sierra stared down at Micah,

who had just caught sight of the mobile overhead. "Who would have guessed we were all lucky to survive childhood with the menace of blankets hanging over us?"

He turned to meet her gaze. "Best to be safe though."

"Of course," she agreed, thinking he might have missed the teasing note in her voice. But then, Colt didn't seem like the sort of man who'd ever made time for laughter and teasing.

For a moment, she had a frivolous hope that she could bring those things into his life over the next few weeks. Then she reminded herself that Colt wasn't her focus here.

She'd only agreed to take the temporary gig for Micah.

"Is it overly optimistic of me to think he's going to sleep?" Colt asked, reaching for the horse mobile to wind it again.

And why were his strong arms so distracting?

"Not at all." She turned away to flip on the baby monitor she'd spotted on a windowsill, then picked up the receiver to pass to Colt.

Only to find him still staring down into the crib.

"I can't believe I'm a father." Colt raked a restless hand through his hair. "It's incredible, and scary as hell at the same time."

Envy for his simple path to parenthood knotted

inside her. Robbing her of breath for a moment. She would give anything for the chance to carry a child.

Still, she tried to reassure him. "I'll bet every first-time parent is a little terrified. And you've had less time than most people to get used to the idea."

"We will be okay." He gripped the crib rail tightly, as if he could make the words true by force of will. "I just feel bad that Micah will have so little family between me being an only child, my parents being gone, and Arielle's passing."

His jaw flexed as he spoke, the tension—the sadness—in his words making her wonder for the first time what might have happened between Colt and Arielle if Micah's mother had lived. The thought that Colt might have worked out a relationship with her for the sake of his child made Sierra feel all the more like an interloper in his world.

"But you're his father. And you're here with him." She laid her hand over his where it rested on the crib rail. "And he'll always have Eve, and his foster family."

Friendly. Comforting.

Or so she thought until Colt's gaze turned to hers in the dim light. Heat sparked and leaped in his eyes.

Her lips parted in surprise at his expression, her breath huffing in and out too quickly at the shifting, invisible current between them.

Did he feel it, too?

"Are you ready for dinner?" he asked, breaking the tension. His words rumbled along her senses, the quiet intimacy feeling like a caress.

She licked her suddenly dry lips.

"Sounds good," she managed, scavenging a polite smile all the while stuffing down the urge to flee the house and the attraction she had no idea how to handle.

This is for Micah.

Colt reminded himself of this over and over during the dinner he shared with Sierra. He'd invited the smart, sexy woman across the dining table into his life strictly for Micah's sake. He knew she was right about keeping a familiar face around his son during this time of tremendous transition. Kids needed that. His son *deserved* that.

But knowing he'd done the right thing in asking Sierra to stay with him didn't make it any easier to adjust to the way she lit up his insides anytime they were in the same room.

Even as he thought it, the fire he'd laid in the hearth snapped and popped, as if the heat he felt for Sierra only added to the blaze near the sturdy farmhouse table he'd set for their meal.

"This is delicious." Sierra sighed happily, seeming wholly occupied with the coq au vin. "And if the meal is an indication of how you cook on a regular basis, feel free to compensate me in dinners any time."

"I'll keep that in mind." He appreciated the way she'd dug into the food and kept the conversation light after the tension that had thrummed between them in the nursery earlier. "But I only learned a couple of dishes from the cook I hired at the Royal Black Winery."

"A French chef taught you how to make this?" She took a sip of the burgundy he'd served with the meal, the firelight casting a warm glow over her skin and her fair hair.

She really was lovely. The pink glow in her cheeks—whether from the warmth of the fire or the wine—made her green eyes even brighter.

"Tastings have an important role in developing a winery's reputation," he explained, toying with the stem of his crystal glass. "And food pairings drive more people to the tastings. So it made sense to hire a professional to handle that part of the business."

"Is this a vintage you serve with the meal at the winery?" She lifted her glass, the burgundy a deep, rich purple. "I know nothing about wine. Although I hope to learn more at the Royal Wine and Roses Festival later this month."

"I saw a flyer for that event," he mused aloud. "It must be something new. And as for this vintage, it's not one of mine. We serve our own Royal Black Malbec with the dish, but I didn't have time to ship a case over." He hadn't taken the time to pack much of anything. The trip had been a blur of sleeplessness and anxiety.

Hell, he was still reeling from the news that he had a son.

"What was it like taking on your grandfather's dream of a winery? Did you know much about it? Did you do a lot of research?" She speared a bite of chicken on her fork before turning her eyes back to him, appearing fully attentive to his answer.

He wondered if she ever turned off that quick mind of hers.

"I had to research a great deal, but I also knew quite a bit from Granddad." He let the memories come, realizing that he was grateful to share them with someone. Grateful to talk about someone who'd meant so much to him. "Back at the Black Ranch house, my grandfather had a room full of black-and-white prints of French wineries. They were photos he'd taken himself as a young man when he'd toured France."

"So you saw those images your whole life," Sierra added, reporter-like as she seemed to shape a story in her mind. "You always knew that was his dream?"

Colt nodded, his chest aching with the old pain that he hadn't pushed his grandfather to leave Royal and make the dream happen. "I knew that Granddad had put off the winery in order to raise his son here in Royal. But once my dad was managing Black Ranch successfully, when I was five years old, my grandfather decided it was time for his second act. He had already made the travel arrangements when he got the news—" Colt paused to clear his throat. "My parents died in a small plane crash. Granddad scrapped the winery plan to raise me."

"Oh, Colt. I'm so sorry." Sierra's hand slid across the table to rest on his, her empathy obvious in her tone. Her touch. "How heartbreaking for you."

He closed his eyes for a moment to sift through the feelings her touch stirred, needing to suppress some of them. Wanting to soak up the others.

"Thank you. They've been gone a long time, and I made peace with their absence. But the grief of losing Granddad—before he had the chance to see the winery I was in the process of buying for him—that still hurts." Which was why he allowed himself to feel the weight of Sierra's cool fingers along the backs of his.

Why he took comfort from her.

"Did he know?" Sierra asked, a blond eyebrow lifting with the question. Her fingers stirred on his, the smallest grazing of her skin over his.

Colt shook his head, wishing he could shake off his regrets as easily. "Unfortunately, no. It was going to be a surprise." He felt her hand squeeze his. Heard her quick intake of breath that no doubt heralded another expression of sympathy that he shouldn't want. "But as much as that hurt, it taught me not to waste time with loved ones."

Sierra's hand slid away from his, and he missed her touch immediately. But her lips curved in a half smile as she seemed to follow his train of thought.

"Clearly you learned the lesson well. You didn't waste a minute once you knew Arielle had a child. You were here less than twenty-four hours later, ready to meet your son." She set aside her fork, her plate cleaned.

In the silence that followed, the fire crackled again. The baby monitor hummed with the sound of Micah making a soft baby sigh. And with Sierra seated across from him, her clear green gaze empathetic and accepting, Colt had a taste of what it might be like to have a woman in his life.

The idea rattled him to his core.

Especially since he had no business thinking about anything like that when he'd already failed his son by indulging his own selfish interests. He'd put his needs ahead of protecting Arielle and Micah.

So he sure as hell didn't trust his judgment where women were concerned.

"I arrived as soon as I could," Colt acknowledged belatedly, his brusque tone chasing the warmth from Sierra's green eyes. "But I'm not sure how long I'll be staying."

He needed to resurrect barriers with this woman. Starting now.

"What do you mean? In the Fenwick house?" Sierra's brow furrowed.

"I mean I won't be staying in the U.S. for long," he explained, certain the impending physical distance would help them maintain an emotional one. "Once Micah has adjusted to me, I'll be taking him back to France. To my home."

Five

Sierra tried not to react outwardly to the bombshell Colt had just launched.

She'd had a lifetime to grapple with the consequences of being an impulsive person, so she recognized that blurting out *hell, no!* would be uncalled for. Unwelcome.

And yet…how could Colt consider plucking Micah out of Royal, Texas, when the town had rallied around the baby all these months?

Gripping her fork with tense fingers, she felt the formerly delicious meal stir uneasily in her belly as she tried to craft an appropriate response to his news.

"I hope you'll reconsider that idea," she said finally, setting aside the fork and pushing her chair further from the table. "Micah has experienced a lot of upheaval in his life between losing his mother and then being taken away from the home and people he's known for the last five months."

"He's my son," Colt reminded her, an edge in his voice as he stood to clear their plates. "He belongs with me."

Sierra hurried to help him, not wanting to alienate Colt now when it might only hasten his departure from Royal. She'd never anticipated that he might wish to leave town with Micah.

"And no one is arguing that. Micah does belong with you." She carried the leftovers to the polished mesquite countertop that looked original to the farmhouse. "But I'm sure you appreciate that a sense of security is tremendously important for a child."

When he didn't answer at first, continuing to clean up after their meal, Sierra pressed, "I'm just suggesting you think about it for a while. Take the time to see how well-loved your son is in this town before you make any more changes in his life. You have to admit he's had a lot of upheaval."

"Understood." Colt's shoulders tightened as he bent forward over the wide, apron-front sink to rinse dishes. "But I also have to make the decision that seems best for my son and me. If that means leaving town to continue building the Royal Black Winery, then that's what I'll do."

Sierra buzzed with unhappy retorts about that, but she stifled each and every one of them, telling herself that Colt was dealing with a lot right now. She'd tamp down her own feelings and return to the subject when she felt calmer.

Yet as she brought their empty wineglasses over to the sink, she couldn't resist asking one more question.

"Why do you like your life in France more than the one you had here?" She couldn't imagine being happy so far from where she'd grown up. She'd traveled around the U.S. to pursue stories for her magazine but had never experienced any great urge to see the world, let alone live far from her birthplace. "Doesn't every native Texan claim the state as home no matter how far they roam?"

She was only half joking.

And fortunately, her words made Colt crack a smile.

"You'll notice I did name the winery after my hometown, so I see your point," he conceded, switching off the hot water before drying his hands on a kitchen towel. He leaned a hip against the countertop. "It's not that I prefer the French countryside to my home. But I haven't finished my work there, and I still intend to make my grandfather's dream a success."

"I see," she forced herself to say, even though she

didn't see at all. The news rattled her, making her too aware that her time with Micah had an expiration date. "Although you must admit, it will make things difficult for me as I care for him every day, knowing all the while I'll only have to say goodbye to him in the end."

How hard would it be to grow more and more attached before Colt moved away?

Colt frowned as he hung the dish towel on the handle to the dishwasher. "I hope you're not reconsidering our arrangement now that you know my plans."

"Of course not," she shot back, not quite managing to hide her frustration. It would certainly be easier to persuade him to stay if she lived here. She folded her arms, staring him down while the fire crackled in the hearth nearby. "I will follow through. In fact, I should probably go home now and organize some of my things to bring over. Should I start tomorrow?"

The relief scrawled across his features was so evident that Sierra felt a small measure of satisfaction that—at least for now—he needed her help. Wanted it.

"The sooner the better. Would you like me to drive you to the B and B? I could ask the ranch foreman's wife to come over for an hour in case Micah wakes while we're gone. I have a truck if you need me to move anything." Straightening from where he'd leaned against the counter, he suddenly seemed closer.

Loomed larger.

Her throat went dry. And how could he have such a potent effect on her when she was still actively upset with his decision to leave Royal?

"No, thank you. I travel lightly and don't have very much." She took a step back, needing some distance. Craving some space to come up with a game plan for dealing with this unwanted attraction.

"Will you come back tonight?" His blue eyes locked on hers, stirring an answering flutter in her chest. "I can show you where you'll be sleeping."

The thought of being in a bed under his roof shouldn't have felt so intimate. It was a simple arrangement for Micah's sake.

And yet…

Her cheeks went warm at the thought of having Colt show her to a bedroom.

She swallowed hard. "That won't be necessary. Micah sleeps through the night now, so you won't have to worry. I think I'll spend the night at the B and B to organize and regroup, then I'll come by in the morning with my things."

He studied her for a long moment before nodding. Then he turned to open a long drawer and withdrew a key tied with a piece of twine. He passed it to her.

"In that case, here's the key." His fingers brushed

her hand. "I appreciate you agreeing to help me, Sierra."

"Of course." She clutched the cold metal into her palm, willing away the tingling sensations his touch had inspired. "I'm looking forward to spending more time with Micah."

She would take every possible moment she could with the little boy, all the while using her time with Colt to convince him to remain in Royal. She couldn't bear to part with Micah, for one thing. But for another? She knew it would be good for Micah to have the love and support of the family and community he had here.

As for the baby's compelling father? Sierra would have to work overtime to keep the boundaries between them despite living under the same roof.

Four days into his arrangement with Sierra as a temporary live-in nanny, Colt seriously questioned his sanity.

He'd stepped out of the calving barn at Black Ranch after checking on a new mother, only to see Sierra at the fence near an outdoor group pen with other pairs of cows and calves. She'd taken to bringing Micah over to see the animals ever since he'd told her the ranch was in calving season.

Which was sweet of her, he admitted. He wanted to see more of his child and also wanted his son to acquire a love of the land.

And clearly Micah enjoyed himself, trying to imitate the animal sounds from his seat in the stroller that Sierra pushed a mile each way from the Fenwick house. So Colt could hardly complain about the activity. Yet he'd taken to working in the barns this week just to breathe in air scented with fresh hay instead of Sierra's orange blossom fragrance.

Having her under his roof was proving far more of a temptation than he'd ever imagined. She stood in his son's darkened room with him at night to put the boy to bed, her hair sometimes brushing Colt's shoulder as she leaned into the crib at the same time as him. She was in his kitchen in the mornings, looking sexy and slightly rumpled in the oversized shirts and shorts she slept in, her hair piled on her head and glasses perched on her nose. She didn't cook, but she bought exotic brands of coffee, making them brews that had more notes than his wines.

Just this morning, she'd informed him that they were drinking something with molasses undertones, and he'd gotten so caught up in listening to the slight rasp of her morning voice that he hadn't heard half of what she'd said. He'd been too busy thinking about waking up beside her.

Which, in turn, sent him running for a day in the barns.

Only to find her here, laughing at something Micah did, her head tipped back as the throaty chuckle escaped. Everything tightened inside him at the sound. Or was it the sight of her, dressed in dark yoga pants that hugged her curves and a loose green tee knotted at her narrow waist? Blond tendrils escaped the ponytail she wore, teasing her cheek in a warm breeze.

Seized by the days of frustration that came from ignoring his personal hungers, Colt strode toward her as if drawn by a magnet.

Green eyes lifted to his as he neared. Her whole body went still, like a wild creature caught out in the open and unsure of its next move. He wanted to answer that uncertainty with the hot persuasion of his touch. His kiss.

But he only jammed his hands in his pockets as he tried not to scowl at her.

"Are we interrupting?" she asked, hugging Micah closer.

The baby played with a loose strand of her hair, watching his chubby fingers wind through the silky piece.

Colt wished he had the right to touch her.

"Of course not." He couldn't help his brusque tone, even knowing how he sounded. Clearing his throat, he tried again. "I appreciate you taking Micah out for some fresh air."

He dragged a boot through the grass near the calving pen, the soft green shoots smelling like spring. Then, realizing she was still holding his son in her arms, Colt reached to take the boy, being careful to untwine Sierra's hair from the baby's fingers first.

The interaction brought them close together and gave Colt a chance to smooth his fingers over that silken strand for himself, even though that hadn't been his objective. Or at least not his main one.

"How's your newest calf doing today?" she asked once Colt had straightened. She shaded her eyes with one hand against the afternoon sunlight. "Did the dam end up accepting her?"

He'd been worried about the heifer even before the difficult birth and he'd shared the story with Sierra over breakfast the day before to avoid thinking about the appealing quality of her morning voice.

"All went well," he assured her, recognizing the soft spot she seemed to have for any abandoned baby—human or otherwise. Harmon Wentworth and Micah weren't the only ones who drew her maternal interest. "We had one of our most knowledgeable ranch hands on duty this morning, and he convinced the mama to lick her calf by pouring some of her feed on the baby. Now the two of them are bonded, and the mama's nursing like a pro."

"I'm glad to hear it." A sunny smile lit her face. "I probably shouldn't have made the walk over here so close to Micah's nap time, but I kept thinking about the calf being rejected."

"We take good care of the animals at Black Ranch." He was a little surprised that the story had lingered with her. "There's not a single ranch hand on staff that doesn't enjoy the springtime with the animals."

"I can see why," she told him softly, her attention shifting back to the new calves and mothers in the group pen. Two of the calves closest to them were running and jumping, demonstrating good social behaviors that meant they'd be ready to join the larger herd soon. "They're so fun to watch."

"Maybe you missed your calling as a rancher," he teased. "You could spend whole days out here." Colt watched her as one of the older cows moved toward the fence, clearly interested in Sierra. "You can pet her if you'd like. She's a veteran mother, not skittish or aggressive."

"Is that what makes a good mother?" she asked, her tone sounding a bit strained as she scratched the cow's neck. "Firsthand experience?"

Colt followed Sierra toward the fence, careful to keep his body between Micah and the animal, no matter how much he trusted her.

"In a cow, it certainly helps." He wanted to see her face to try and read her expression, but she tipped her forehead into the animal's neck, remaining hidden for a long moment.

Had he missed something?

He stayed alert to her until she straightened again, her face cleared. Neutral. But sadder, somehow. The earlier laughter and sunny smile were gone.

"I should be getting Micah back home." Moving away from the fence, she headed toward the stroller. "Would you mind buckling him in for me?"

He followed behind her with the baby. "Is everything all right? Did I say something—"

"Everything's fine," she said in a voice that seemed too bright. Leaning over the stroller, she cleared aside the straps to give Colt a clear path for his son. "I'd just better hurry before Micah gets hungry for his afternoon bottle. I lost track of the time."

"Why don't I drive you both home?" he suggested gently, sensing something was off with Sierra even if she didn't want to admit it. "My truck's right over there. There's already a car seat in the back."

He pointed to the heavy-duty model he kept at Black Ranch for work. He'd taken it out of storage earlier in the week to supervise operations as long as he was home.

Her green eyes clouded as she hesitated. For a moment she appeared so troubled that Colt was tempted to do something foolish like pull her against him and demand to know what was wrong. What had upset her?

Micah patted his shoulder with his tiny hands, the fingers clenching and unclenching rhythmically against Colt's T-shirt.

"I could use a few minutes to myself, actually,"

she finally said. "Would you mind bringing Micah back while I—take a little time?"

She looked so vulnerable in that instant that he had no choice but to ignore the tug of his own curiosity. He would have done whatever she asked.

"Of course I will." He knew she'd shouldered more of the baby care this week than he had, in part because he'd been running hard and fast from his attraction to her. Had he inadvertently asked too much of her? Guilt pinched him. "Take whatever time you need. I can load up Micah and give him his next bottle."

"Thank you." Her voice was rough. The rasp was back, and not in the way that had driven him out of his mind with desire this morning. Now she sounded rattled, and it gutted him to think he could be at fault.

"Sierra, I'm sorry if I've been leaving too much to you—"

But she'd already spun on the heel of her tennis shoe to hurry away up the dirt road that acted as a shortcut between the Fenwick and Black lands.

Damn it.

"Should we check on her?" he asked aloud to Micah. His temple throbbed with the sudden knowledge that he might have pushed the limits of what a transplanted reporter was ready to handle as a nanny this week.

"Moo," Micah told him, his little face serious as

he stared back at the enclosed pasture full of calves and cows. "Moo moo."

Colt's chest filled with pride at the sound that may have been just lucky timing but felt more like a stroke of baby genius.

"That's right, big guy. The cows say moo." Colt hugged the boy tighter to him, planting a kiss on his downy-soft forehead.

"Moo moo," Micah seemed to correct him as he laid his dark curls on Colt's shoulder.

"You know best," Colt conceded, pushing the stroller toward his truck with one hand while he kept Micah secured in the other. "I admire that you stand your ground like that."

With one last glance over his shoulder to where Sierra had vanished into the woods separating the properties, Colt lifted the stroller into his truck bed before opening the rear door to settle Micah in the baby car seat.

"Moo moo?" the boy asked, sitting up straighter when it would have been helpful for buckling purposes to have him relax into the seat.

Micah's dark eyes were wide. Curious.

"We've got to leave them now, buddy," Colt soothed his son, guiding one leg through a seat strap. "We're going to head home now."

He was anxious to talk to Sierra once Micah was settled in for a nap. Find out what was troubling her. Maybe it had something to do with her work. The book she was writing on the Texas Cattleman's Club or a story she was tracking down. He hadn't asked her anything about her work since she'd moved into his house, his focus on Micah and—of course— avoiding the attraction to Sierra.

"Moo moo!" Micah's word became an adamant demand. An argument, really. His body was stiff. Unrelenting.

And very, very difficult to buckle into a car seat.

"We'll see them tomorrow," Colt consoled, wondering how a tiny body could exert so much force straightening itself out when Colt needed him to bend a little. Micah's body was like a plank. "But right now we're going back to the house to make sure Sierra is okay."

Dark eyes turned toward him. There was a momentary loss of focus on straining away from the car seat straps.

"You want to see Sierra?" Colt asked, wondering if the boy could possibly recognize her name. But then, hadn't Micah just shown some baby genius tendencies a minute ago? "I wouldn't blame you, you know. I need to see her, too."

Seeming to sigh with resignation, Micah relaxed into the soft cotton fabric of the car seat. Colt channeled his old calf-roping skills to weave the straps into their proper places, snapping, tucking and buckling in record time. He wasn't taking any chances that his son was going to repeat the planking routine.

Moments later, Colt was on the road back to the Fenwick house. He wouldn't take the pickup over the old dirt road that was a shortcut for two reasons. The ride would be less bumpy for Micah on pavement. Plus, Colt wasn't about to creep up on Sierra when he'd promised her some space.

He would return to the house, feed Micah and then think about what he could do to give Sierra a break. He could cook dinner tonight of course. So far she'd joined him for evening meals.

Lately they'd used those dinners as a way to discuss Micah. Colt had been absorbing all she knew about babies, including all she knew about Micah. Over the last few days he'd been able to hear the full story of the hunt for first Micah's mother and then—when they'd discovered Arielle's death and Eve Martin's heart condition that had briefly incapacitated her—the search for him.

But Colt was caught up now. He'd made peace with his feelings about Arielle, because even if he'd been upset that she hadn't contacted him initially about their child, he couldn't be more grateful for the amazing kid she'd brought into the world. He had a better sense of how to care for his son than he had earlier in the week. Tonight, he was turning his attention to Sierra and whatever was troubling her today. Maybe he could help her find a way to relax. He had an idea for something she might like, too.

Because even though he had no intention of acting on the attraction between them, he realized that he absolutely didn't want to see her upset. He'd been serious about owing her more than he could ever repay. She'd made the connection between him and Micah that no one else had caught. If not for her, he wouldn't have known he had a son in the world.

His gaze went to the rearview mirror. Micah's dark eyes were already half-closed, his round cheeks pink from the outdoor air. A wave of tenderness rolled over him along with that ever-present guilt that he hadn't known about the boy just one week ago.

So yes, he'd do anything in his power to make things right for Sierra again.

Six

"I can't believe I'm going fishing," Sierra mused aloud as she stared out of Colt's pickup truck window toward the Brazos River meandering lazily in front of them.

Just two hours had passed since she'd had to leave the calving barn after a fit of emotions had overcome her. Colt would never guess how his comment about mothering in cows had tweaked Sierra's frustrated maternal feelings. She certainly didn't blame him for upsetting her. She'd just needed some space after an exhausting week of working on her book while Micah slept.

By the time she'd returned to the farmhouse, she'd felt a little steadier. Ready to continue with her baby caretaking duties. But Colt had surprised her with an impromptu fishing outing and picnic instead, having already arranged for Eve Martin and Rafael Wentworth to babysit Micah for a few hours since he was familiar with them.

"I know you mentioned needing some time to yourself," Colt explained as he switched off the truck and withdrew the keys. He turned toward her from his spot in the driver's seat. "But it occurred to me that fishing is the perfect way to have a mental and emotional retreat even when you're with other people. It's one of the reasons I renew my fishing license every year. I enjoy the quiet."

She tore her gaze from the winding strip of blue that babbled quietly between hills. "I'm game. Even if your idea of quiet and mine are probably worlds apart."

"Afraid I'll make too much noise?" he asked as he opened the driver's side door.

She couldn't help but laugh. Especially as she considered that had been the whole reason he'd said it. He'd wanted to make her smile. And as the more vocal of the two of them, Sierra didn't mind being called out about her voice.

"Maybe. But I'm sure you'll try your best to keep it down." Still grinning, she followed him out of the vehicle and around to the cargo bed, where Colt was already lifting a picnic basket and blanket from the back. "How can I help?"

Colt picked up a tackle box and carried the silver container in his free hand. "No need. Why don't you pick a spot for us to spread out the blanket?"

Frowning, she searched the truck bed with her gaze. "I can at least carry the fishing poles."

She gripped them in one hand before raising the rods free of the lift gate.

"How about here?" Colt called, setting down the hamper and denting the tall grass as he gestured toward a spot under a river birch.

She breathed in the fresh air and clean scent of spring, the leaves newly green in the trees all around them. The banks were softly rolling, not high, but not flat either. It was a pretty piece of countryside, well off the county route. There were no other cars around, or houses for that matter, although down below them, she could see two kayakers paddling silently downriver.

"Is this spot close enough to the water?" She set down the poles against the birch's narrow trunk, shading her eyes from the late day sun reflecting off the water. "I don't have any experience casting from a bank. I've only been fishing one other time, and that was from a canoe."

She couldn't help watching him spread out the faded blue quilt, the muscles in his broad back shifting with his movements beneath the close-fitting black Henley shirt. He'd showered after his work in the barns, and his hair had still been damp when they'd started their drive to the Brazos River. Now the dark strands lifted in the breeze off the water, making her wonder what it would feel like to comb her fingers through them.

"We'll be fine. I've got full spools and light lines on the rods, so a nice long cast won't be a problem." He waved her closer. "Come and have a seat."

For a moment, she hesitated. Everything about Colt Black and this afternoon trip enticed her. Hadn't she wanted to avoid one-on-one time with him just because she found him so appealing? Yet she'd accepted the invitation, seizing on the chance to forget the unexpected hurt she'd grappled with back at the calving shed. She'd been glad for the chance to redirect her thoughts and escape the muddle of her emotions.

Even if it meant throwing herself into a picnic that felt sort of like a date. She ambled closer to the quilt and dropped down to sit on one side.

"Your answer makes me think you must know a few things about fishing," she observed, tipping her head back to enjoy the feel of the spring sunshine on her face while he carried the fishing poles over to the blanket. "Is there anything you can't do? Cooking, winemaking, ranching, fishing—"

"Whoa. To say I've got more than casual cooking skills is an affront to any seasoned homemaker." He lowered himself to sit beside her, dragging the tackle box to rest between them. "And as for winemaking, I employ people who know what they're doing while I try to educate myself."

Head bent to the task of choosing lures, Colt seemed lighter out here. As if he were genuinely enjoying himself in a way that she hadn't observed before today. Prior to this afternoon, she'd had the impression he'd been avoiding her whenever she was alone. He was always ready, eager even, to help with Micah. Or to talk over issues related to his son. But Colt had never lingered in her presence when the baby wasn't with them.

Until now. Was there any chance he was enjoying Royal more? Any chance he would consider staying in town instead of taking Micah halfway around the world to live in a French winery? It was in her best interests to ensure Colt remembered the things he enjoyed best about his birthplace. All the more reason to stay right here, where he seemed at home.

"If you learn winemaking as quickly as you've taken to baby care, then I'm sure you're doing well." She traced the shape of the rod and reel, observing for herself the full spool while the sound of a backfiring truck engine sounded from the county route in the distance.

Colt lifted his head from his task, his blue eyes lasering in on hers. "Thank you, Sierra. That means a lot to me. Well, *Micah* means everything to me," he amended. "So it only follows that I'd want to figure out how to be the best possible parent. I appreciate you helping me."

His honesty appealed to her as much as his love for his son. Colt Black hid a tender heart for his child underneath his very serious and driven exterior.

"I'm glad I could do this," she admitted, hoping this time together would help her convince him to remain in Royal. She couldn't imagine parting with Micah. "It worked out well that I took a break from the magazine to write a book. I wouldn't have been able to stay otherwise."

"Your commitment to Micah is obvious." He returned to his work, tying the end of one line around the lure he'd chosen before passing her the rod. "Do you feel comfortable casting on your own?"

"I'd need instructions." She peered over at him. "I wouldn't want to impale anyone on a fishhook."

"Of course." He shifted closer to her on the quilt, putting them almost shoulder to shoulder. "Take your pole, and I'll demonstrate on mine first."

Lifting the smaller pole, she followed his motions as he let out a few feet of line. The lure—a skinny fake fish of some kind—dragged against her ankle where her three-quarter-length jeans didn't cover the skin above her tennis shoes.

"Now what?" she asked, checking the length of his line compared to hers.

"Then press here, like you're holding a trigger. That's going to allow the line to unspool when you cast." He demonstrated this, too.

And although her attention should have been on

his hands, her focus snagged on his lightly bristled jaw, and the strong column of his throat that disappeared into the collar of his shirt.

"Okay," she nodded absently, thinking she could watch him all day. "I'm ready."

Maybe something in her tone gave away her careful perusal of him, because he glanced over at her again, his blue eyes darkening as they met hers.

Sparks leaped. Her breath caught.

Yet Colt returned his attention the river below the bank.

"Now, we're ready to let it fly." Rising to his feet, he swung the fishing rod back over one shoulder before flinging it effortlessly toward the current. The line spun out, a shiny white filament that caught the sunlight for a moment before the lure splashed down into the middle of the water.

"Nice job," she murmured as she stood.

She didn't allow her gaze to return to the man beside her. Taking a deep breath, she cocked back the rod, remembering the way he'd flicked it forward to cast. For a moment, she watched the way the line unspooled, free and unfettered. The same as she'd been these last years since finding out her condition wouldn't allow her to have children.

But was she really free when her sadness about that weighted her down? When the hurt returned to twist her gut like it had earlier today at the barn when Colt mentioned what made for a good mother?

Colt whistled low and long. "Like a pro."

It took her a moment to realize he'd been admiring the cast while she'd been grappling with her demons. Demons that had started to make her feel more alone—lonely—than free.

After planting his fishing rod into the soft earth in front of the blanket so he didn't have to hold it, Colt took hers and repeated the action with the second pole. All the while, her eyes followed him hungrily.

Did he sense her stare? Her preoccupation with him? At least a dozen times a day she thought about him telling her that he was attracted to her. Wondered what might happen between them if they weren't trying to avoid the complications of acting on it.

Being with him reminded her of the months—years—she'd gone without a man's touch. A man's kiss. Funny that she had scarcely missed that intimacy until Colt strode into her life.

"Now we wait," he announced, settling back onto the quilt while she sat beside him. Not quite as close as before, but still near enough to make her aware of his warmth.

His strength.

Especially when he propped himself on one elbow, his whole body reclining as he tipped his face to the sun.

He propped an eyelid open after a moment, catching her staring at him. "Are you going to tell me what's on your mind, Sierra?"

His low voice rumbled through her. She felt it like a chord reverberating through her belly, humming long afterward. She didn't want to talk about what was bothering her. So she made herself more comfortable on the quilt, imitating his posture and propping herself on one elbow. Facing him.

"Right now?" She lowered her eyes to admire the shape of his mouth, appealingly close to hers. "Only one thing."

She felt his sharp intake of breath along her lips. A phantom kiss she longed to capture. Taste.

But instead of his mouth, she felt his knuckle under her chin, tipping her face so she had to meet his gaze. The heat simmering in those blue depths made her heartbeat quicken.

"Tell me." The words, though softly spoken, were a demand.

Would anything less have coaxed the truth from her?

She scavenged up her courage.

"I need you to kiss me, Colt. Right now. For as long as possible."

He didn't think twice.

Hell, he didn't even think one time.

Colt heard what she wanted—no, *needed*—and drew her closer to provide it. Releasing her chin, he slid his hand around to the small of her back and tucked her against him.

She stared at him with wide green eyes right up until the moment he grazed her lower lip with his. Then he watched her long lashes flutter and fall closed, her hand lifting to rest lightly on his chest.

She must have felt his heart thundering like a herd released to a fresh pasture. Must have known the effect she was having on him. He'd tried his best to lock it down. But today he'd seen a different side of her. A vulnerable one. Between that and her admission of the same attraction that had been eating at him night and day ever since they'd met, Colt couldn't possibly deny what they both craved.

Especially with her mouth so soft, so giving against his. He wanted to take his time. Feast on her. But her whole body responded to the kiss, a shiver tripping up her spine that he could feel where he touched her. Her hips rocked toward him, and he was pretty sure he saw fireworks behind his eyelids.

The need to roll her to her back, to cover her and feel every inch of her against him, was a new fire in his blood. It flared hot and greedy, which made it all the more imperative that he took no more than the kiss.

But damn, he would have his way with her sweet, sexy mouth.

Slanting his lips over hers, he licked his way inside. She tasted better than any world-class vintage he'd ever rolled around his palate. Sierra was more nuanced. Complex. One moment, her head tipped against the quilt to give him full access, submitting to the play of his tongue over hers. And the next, she raked her fingers through his hair to anchor herself to him, demanding more, answering each lick with one of her own.

He broke apart to give them air. To allow a cooling breath to tame the heat rising between them.

"Sierra." He growled her name against her damp mouth, unable to move any farther away from her than a fraction of an inch. "I'm doing my damnedest to keep this just a kiss."

Her breath huffed warm against his cheek. They were so close that her breasts pressed his chest with every inhale. The need to wrap his arms around her and seal their bodies together had his hands twitching. The rest of him aching.

"And you're doing an excellent job of it." She curved her palm around his jaw, her fingers stroking along his cheekbone, her thumb sliding over his lower lip. "I can't remember the last time I had a kiss this good."

Her green eyes were passion-dazed, her focus returning to his mouth. Logically, he guessed she was hiding from something that upset her by acting on this attraction now. But he saw the appeal. How much would he rather lose himself in a kiss than face his real problems?

His unworthiness to be a father, for example,

since he hadn't been around for Micah for the first six months of his son's life?

"Uh-oh." Sierra went still beneath him. "What's wrong?"

He closed his eyes for a moment, regretting that he'd allowed the thoughts to show on his face.

"I'm sorry." He eased away, putting space between them even though he would have preferred to dive back into the heat and connection between them. "Sometimes the realization of what I've done—putting a continent between me and my son during half of one of the most formative years of his life—"

He broke off, unable to complete the thought. Sitting up, he stared out at the Brazos River and the two motionless fishing poles standing sentinel on either side of their quilt.

"You're off to an amazing start at being a good dad, Colt." Sierra's voice beside him made him aware she'd straightened, too. She stared out at the water with him, her arms looping around knees drawn up to her chin. "You know how I know?"

Her blond hair blew onto his shoulder in the light breeze, a barely there touch.

Still, he couldn't answer. Wasn't sure he could grapple with this now when the anger at himself kept him awake at night. What if Sierra hadn't found him?

"I was abandoned as a child," she said finally, continuing even though he hadn't spoken.

Her words stunned him. His head whipped around to gauge her expression. Her face was set in unfamiliar lines, an old pain scrawled in her features somehow.

"I'm sorry—" he began, but she waved off the words with a shake of her head.

"It was a long time ago. But my story isn't all that different from Micah's. Except instead of showing up on the trunk of a car, I was found on a church doorstep in Houston's Third Ward when I was three weeks old." She turned to face him, tilting her temple onto her knee as she spoke. "I didn't tell anyone in Royal about that. But that's why I got so involved in Micah's life."

Her vigilance. Her relentless pursuit of the truth. Her quests to connect parents to children that— according to Cammie Wentworth—had been more effective than efforts by the police—made all the more sense.

"No wonder you bonded with my son." Then a pang ripped through his chest. "Although I can't stand the idea that Micah will tell that same story one day. That he was found abandoned and alone."

She lifted her head again, giving it an emphatic shake as it to refute his point though.

"He won't. And that's my whole point in telling you my story now. I never had a reunion with my parents. They never claimed me. And believe me, I searched for them as hard as I searched for you." Her jaw tensed, lips pursing. But then she seemed to huff out the tension, her shoulders easing a fraction and her voice softening as she continued. "The difference is they truly did abandon me. Whereas you came as soon as you knew there was even a chance that you had a child. And *no one* can fault you for that."

He wouldn't have dared to argue with her. Not with that fierceness in her tone, or that flashing of challenge in her eyes. He released a long breath of his own, feeling some of the anger at himself fade. Not all. But some.

"Thank you for that." He smoothed a wrinkle in the quilt between them, wishing it were as easy to smooth away the obstacles between them. To return to the simplicity of kissing on a warm spring day. "I know you only shared the story for my sake, but I can't help wondering how things went for you after you were found as an infant. Were you adopted?"

"I was. It happened within a few weeks, too, and my adoptive parents are kick-ass. They were older, and I was their only child, so they made me the center of their world." A smile pulled her lips up. "They still do."

"I'm glad." He wanted to stroke a hand over her hair, smooth the strands and pull her against him at the same time. But he knew that falling back into the kiss was a bad idea.

Not only because he wasn't ready for any relationship. Also because she'd never told him what had upset her earlier, back at the calving barn. Would she share it with him now?

She remained quiet beside him, so he ventured, "Can I ask you one more thing?"

Her left eyebrow raised in question as she turned to look at him again. "I thought I was the reporter? Are you going to repay me in kind and let me ask you questions afterward?"

He refused to be deterred, however. Not when it seemed important.

"What happened at the calving shed earlier today? I keep going over it, and I'm still not sure what went wrong."

Her gaze shuttered. Expression closed off.

He knew right away that she wasn't going to answer him.

Lifting her chin, she turned toward the water again. Only to grip his knee a moment later.

"Colt!" She pointed at her fishing pole, eyes wide. "I think I got a bite."

Seven

A week after her fishing trip with Colt, Sierra continued to replay the kiss they'd shared. Even now as she sat working alone in the living room of the renovated Fenwick house—long after she'd tucked Micah in bed for the night—she couldn't concentrate on her notes regarding Violetta Ford for thinking about Colt.

How he'd tasted. How he'd touched her. How kind he'd been to plan an outing for her when she'd been feeling overwhelmed.

Tipping her head back into the leather couch cushion, she sat in front of a fire she'd started after Micah had gone to bed. A rainstorm had brought cooler temperatures for the past two days, and Sierra welcomed the warmth of the blaze as she closed her eyes to relive the kiss once more. At least, she hoped it was just once more, since she recognized that she had to stop thinking about her temporary employer that way.

She'd successfully avoided romantic relationships for four years to keep her fertility woes on lockdown, unwilling to weigh someone else down with a disappointment that was all her own. Yes, she could adopt. And maybe one day she would. But for now, she was all about her work.

Or she had been, until one kiss from Colt got her thinking about the joys of being with a man. And wow, she'd forgotten how good it could be to be wrapped in someone's arms and kissed like there was no tomorrow. Then again, maybe she hadn't missed a man's kiss all that much because no one had ever made her feel quite as delicious as Colt had last week.

Behind her, the front door to the house opened, startling her eyes open as the sound of a sharp gust whistled through the foyer.

She had a clear view of the entryway, where the man she'd been thinking about stepped onto the welcome mat, his black Stetson and oilskin duster still sluicing rain onto the floor. Her insides clutched at the sight of him, his wide shoulders angling away from her as he slid off the wet coat and hung it on a hook above a waterproof floor mat. His hat went on another hook before he toed off his boots.

With his hat gone, she could see his profile more clearly. The strong jaw. The slash of brows and prominent cheekbones. The lips that had molded so tenderly to her own.

"You must be glad to be out of the rain," she observed softly, suspecting he hadn't noticed her yet.

His head whipped around, taking her in. Expression turning troubled?

Something in his face made her wonder if he'd been avoiding her again. But then, she understood the impulse well enough. It was easier not to act on an attraction if they were never alone together.

"I'm sorry. I didn't see you there," he explained, swiping his forearm across his face, no doubt to dry off the lingering damp. His gray work shirt and jeans appeared dry, however. "How did things go with Micah today?"

She wrenched her gaze up from where his jeans hugged strong thighs. Colt still participated in as much of Micah's care as he could, but Sierra knew he had work to attend as well. Continuing renovations around the Fenwick ranch kept him busy some of the time, but he also had regular online meetings with his staff at the winery and duties on Black Ranch. She suspected the latter had kept him out in the rain this afternoon instead of putting Micah to bed with her.

Treat Yourself with 2 Free Books!

Sizzling Romance

Passionate Romance

GET UP TO 4 FREE BOOKS & 2 FREE GIFTS WORTH OVER $20

See Inside For Details

Claim Them While You Can

Get ready to relax and indulge with your FREE BOOKS and more!

Claim up to FOUR NEW BOOKS & TWO MYSTERY GIFTS – absolutely FREE!

Dear Reader,

We both know life can be difficult at times. That's why it's important to treat yourself so you can relax and recharge once in a while.

And I'd like to help you do this by sending you this amazing offer of up to FOUR brand new full length FREE BOOKS that WE pay for.

This is everything I have ready to send to you right now:

Try **Harlequin® Desire** books featuring the worlds of the American elite with juicy plot twists, delicious sensuality and intriguing scandal.

Try **Harlequin Presents® Larger-Print** books featuring the glamorous lives of royals and billionaires in a world of exotic locations, where passion knows no bounds.

Or **TRY BOTH!**

All we ask in return is that you answer 4 simple questions on the attached Treat Yourself survey. You'll get **Two Free Books** and **Two Mystery Gifts** from each series you try, *altogether worth over $20*! Who could pass up a deal like that?

Sincerely,

Pam Powers

Harlequin Reader Service

Treat Yourself to Free Books and Free Gifts.

Answer 4 fun questions and get rewarded.

We love to connect with our readers!
Please tell us a little about you...

	YES	NO
1. I LOVE reading a good book.	○	○
2. I indulge and "treat" myself often.	○	○
3. I love getting FREE things.	○	○
4. Reading is one of my favorite activities.	○	○

TREAT YOURSELF • Pick your 2 Free Books...

Yes! Please send me my Free Books from each series I select and Free Mystery Gifts. I understand that I am under no obligation to buy anything, as explained on the back of this card.

Which do you prefer?
- ❏ **Harlequin Desire®** 225/326 HDL GRAN
- ❏ **Harlequin Presents® Larger-Print** 176/376 HDL GRAN
- ❏ **Try Both** 225/326 & 176/376 HDL GRAY

FIRST NAME   LAST NAME

ADDRESS

APT.#   CITY

STATE/PROV.   ZIP/POSTAL CODE

EMAIL ❏ Please check this box if you would like to receive newsletters and promotional emails from Harlequin Enterprises ULC and its affiliates. You can unsubscribe anytime.

▲ If offer card is missing write to: Harlequin Reader Service, P.O. Box 1341, Buffalo, NY 14240-8531 or visit www.ReaderService.com ▲

BUSINESS REPLY MAIL
FIRST-CLASS MAIL   PERMIT NO. 717   BUFFALO, NY

POSTAGE WILL BE PAID BY ADDRESSEE

HARLEQUIN READER SERVICE
PO BOX 1341
BUFFALO NY 14240-8571

NO POSTAGE
NECESSARY
IF MAILED
IN THE
UNITED STATES

"He was a little less fussy today. I called the pediatrician about all the drooling, and she thinks he's just teething again." She set her laptop computer on the low cocktail table so she could turn more fully toward Colt. "I put a couple of teething rings in the fridge, and he really liked gnawing on them."

She'd felt so relieved when he gummed the cold toy, his frustrated cries ceasing for what seemed like the first time in hours.

"Thank you for doing that." Colt strode deeper into the room, his steps silent in sock-clad feet. "And I appreciate you starting a fire. It's a miserable night out there."

He took a seat on the opposite end of the couch from her, the leather creaking as he stretched his feet toward the hearth. She cleared away the notebook and pen from the cushion between them, stacking them on her laptop. It wasn't until she tucked her legs under her and faced him that she realized how domestic the moment felt, sharing the couch at the end of a long workday.

Or maybe it was the way she couldn't keep her eyes off him that kindled the sense of them as a couple. Butterflies fluttered in her stomach.

"I thought you would have been back long ago. Especially because of the rain." She picked at a loose thread at the cuff of a favorite white fisherman's sweater. She hadn't brought many warm clothes to Royal, but today she'd been glad for this.

"I was sorry to miss putting Micah to bed, but we discovered a problem with the irrigation system when we couldn't shut it off." He shook his head, his expression dejected. "One of the hay fields flooded, but at least we found the problem."

"No wonder you're glad for the fire." She shivered just thinking about standing in muddy fields in the downpour. "And bedtime went well. I think Micah was tired out from the teething, and he settled down pretty quickly."

"If it wore him out, I bet it was draining for you, too," he observed, then nodded toward her notes. "I'm surprised you had enough energy to work on your book afterward. I apologize if I've asked too much of you."

The butterflies that had been flitting inside her slowed down. She'd been dreading talking about her project, aware that Colt still viewed her work with skepticism. She wanted to search the Fenwick house and grounds for Violetta's old diary that the woman's ranch hand, Emmalou Hilliard, had assured her was hidden there. She hadn't told Colt that she had checked over some of the outbuildings when she took Micah out for walks in the stroller.

Her gaze darted to the notebook, but she hadn't made any notations about the diary there. Beside her papers, the nursery monitor sat, switched on but silent.

"Sometimes I get a second wind when I start

working," she said carefully, uncertain how much to share. Even more unsure how to tell him that she hoped the Fenwick property would yield the final key to Violetta's story. "And I've really enjoyed finding out as much as I can about Violetta's life. I can't imagine how much courage it took for her to deceive the world as a man just so she could claim a spot in the Texas Cattleman's Club."

The formerly men-only club had refused membership to Violetta, even though she'd run a successful ranch single-handedly in Royal. So Violetta "sold" the ranch to Vincent Fenwick and then disappeared. Vincent was admitted to the TCC almost immediately after moving into the place, a fact that must have made Violetta feel both proud and yet frustrated that she couldn't have achieved the feat on her own merits.

"I didn't know anything about the story when I met with Arielle," Colt mused, surprising her with the direction of his thoughts.

"In all of the drama that came with your arrival in Royal, I almost forgot that's how the two of you met." She propped an elbow on the low back of the leather sofa, warming to the subject. "No one would have unearthed Violetta's story without Arielle's help. Her notes directed Tate Wentworth to letters about Violetta and Dean Wentworth, and how their secret affair led to Harmon Wentworth's birth."

Harmon had seemed relieved to finally know

the story of his birth mother. Sierra's role had been small enough, but she had helped drive things forward with her determination to unearth the secret by talking to everyone in town. She felt pleased that she'd been able to provide closure on the mystery that Arielle's diary had first revealed. For Sierra, it felt like a debt paid, considering how much joy she had in being a part of Micah's life.

"Arielle would have liked you." Colt stared into the flames still burning high and bright. "She was passionate about small-town tales, and although she was looking into a career as a photojournalist, it wasn't just the photos that captivated her. She liked the stories behind them."

For a moment, Sierra's gut cinched with a pang of jealousy for Arielle and what she'd shared with Colt. But she forced away the feeling immediately, angry at herself for coveting anything from a woman who'd died far too soon. Sierra knew Arielle would have traded anything for the chance to see her son grow up.

"I'm going to dedicate my book on Violetta and the TCC to Arielle," she confided, glad she would have some public way to acknowledge the contributions of the other woman.

Colt turned to her, the warmth of his blue gaze sending a shower of sparks through her as he extended his arm across the back of the couch, close to hers. "That's a great idea. And it's a coincidence that you mentioned this, because I was thinking when I finish the renovations on the Fenwick barns, I might ask Carson Wentworth if he'd like to name the stables in honor of Violetta and Dean."

She clapped a hand over Colt's wrist in her enthusiasm.

"You should," she insisted, knowing Carson would be gratified by the gesture, as would Carson's one-hundred-year-old great-grandfather, Harmon. "What a nice way to remember them."

As soon as she touched him, the companionable mood shifted subtly. Heat zinged up her fingers and into her arm. She made a move to draw back, but Colt flipped his wrist over so that he could capture her palm in his.

Surprised at the contact, she glanced down to where their hands joined, her heart racing. Butterflies returned in full force. A butterfly army.

"Sierra." Her name was a gravelly plea, the deep tone of his voice making her breath catch. "I've tried to give you space since…the day we went fishing."

She swallowed hard, not sure she was ready to talk about that kiss. Or why she hadn't been willing to answer his question regarding what had upset her the day she'd visited the calving shed with Micah.

"Thank you," she murmured, even though she wasn't certain she wanted space from him when memories of Colt's mouth on hers set fire to her every time she recalled it.

Even now, her pulse throbbed beneath the place where his hand rested, his long fingers lightly circling her wrist.

"But I'd be lying if I said I didn't enjoy that time with you." He paused the gentle circling to stroke one fingertip down the center of her forearm. "Not only the kiss, although that was a definite highlight. I liked just being with you."

She shivered from that simple touch, a wave of longing crashing through her while the wind and rain howled outside. Being with Colt made her feel…so many things. Too many things.

It was easiest to concentrate on the physical part since that kind of attraction was the simplest to walk away from afterward. Wasn't it? She feared she'd been so far out of the dating loop that she had no idea how to navigate romantic emotions anymore. Nothing about her attraction to Colt felt simple.

"I enjoyed it, too," she confessed, since he must feel her response to him anyhow. "But I remember that first night you asked me to be Micah's temporary nanny, you mentioned—"

"I recall," he interrupted, his tone grim as he withdrew his hand from where it held hers. "I assured you I wouldn't be acting on the attraction I felt for you. I shouldn't have—"

She retrieved his hand, squeezing.

"But you didn't," she rushed to remind him, unwilling for him to shoulder any burden for the turn things had taken on the bank of the Brazos River.

He went still at her touch, listening even though the corners of his mouth turned down.

"*I* asked *you* for the kiss, so if anyone is to blame, it's me," she explained, remembering all too well how they'd ended up in a lip-lock that day. "Only afterward did I let myself think about how you'd drawn that line between us from the start and I hate to think I blurred the boundaries by acting on the… er…" She gestured back and forth between them. "Chemistry."

His expression softened. He leaned closer, bringing the scent of rain and pine trees with him as his voice lowered. "You didn't hear me complaining. I wanted you then. I want you now."

Her heart leaped into her throat. Stayed there. Why did Colt have this potent effect on her? She didn't know what to say, could only stare back at him in a kind of rapt fascination.

"Talk to me, Sierra. What do you want to happen between us?" He slid his free hand around her neck, fingers sifting through the hair while his thumb stroked her cheek.

Could she claim a night for herself with him? The idea had smoked around the edges of her thoughts for days, tempting her. Teasing her.

"I don't want to risk my chance to spend time with Micah," she found herself saying, before she'd even realized that had been a concern from deep within.

"I would never do that to him. Or you." The sincerity in his voice rang true. "You've been a constant in his life."

She wanted to remind him that if Micah stayed in the U.S., he'd have more constants, but she didn't think it was the right time to drag out that argument. For now, she appreciated hearing that Colt saw her that way. That he respected the bond she'd developed to his son.

"Thank you. He means a lot to me." Leaning into Colt's touch, she allowed herself the pleasure of his strong hands on her. Her pulse quickened, heat stirring inside her.

Was she really considering this?

"So we agree you are an important person to Micah." Colt's thumb lowered from her cheek toward her mouth. Gently, he grazed the pad over her lips. "But you still haven't answered my question."

Sierra might have scooted closer to him on the couch. The space between their bodies seemed to shrink, the air in the room thick with longing. Colt was a good man. She trusted him with her body. And more than that? He didn't want a relationship any more than she did. His time with Arielle had left him reeling.

Surely they could enjoy each other this once without worrying about what tomorrow would bring.

"Remind me." Her voice sounded like someone else's. Scratchy with need. "What was the question again?"

All she could think about was closing the rest of the distance between them. Seeing if Colt's kiss felt as good as she remembered.

He tipped his forehead to hers. Their breath mingled. Chests heaving like they'd been running.

"What do you want to happen next, Sierra? It's one hundred percent your call."

Colt didn't trust himself to make the right decision. Not when he needed her this badly. Not when he'd thought about her night and day ever since that kiss had knocked him for a loop a week ago.

Better to let her direct what happened next.

Or maybe he just hoped for a replay of that time at the river when she'd ordered him to kiss her for as long as possible. He would enjoy a command like that. Hell, he craved it. Because telling himself she was off-limits hadn't worked. Reminding himself he'd screwed up in the worst imaginable way with Arielle hadn't been enough to squelch the desire for Sierra either, and he'd tried his damnedest to keep that failing in mind.

Still, he wanted her.

But until he knew that Sierra returned the feeling, he took pleasure from his fingers in the hair tucked behind her ear, his thumb stretched to trace the plump fullness of her gorgeous lips.

He was more worked up just *talking* to her than he'd been for women he'd taken to his bed. Even now, he dragged in deep breaths to catch her scent, the orange blossom fragrance of her skin an aphrodisiac that made him desperate to taste her. She looked so beautiful tonight, her pale hair limned by the firelight, the white cable knit sweater and leggings she wore not doing anything to hide feminine curves.

Finding her in his living room after a hellish day had felt like a reward he didn't deserve. He hoped she wanted him even half as much as he yearned to touch her. All of her.

Before Sierra spoke, she edged back to look him in the eyes, her hands coming to rest on his shoulders.

"I've had a whole week to think about what I want to happen next." Her green gaze never wavered from his as her fingers clenched the fabric of his work shirt. "And now that you've asked, I have a long list."

Heat streaked through him, turning him hard as steel. Sweat popped along his shoulders. His mouth went dry.

"Tell me. Everything." His fingers cupped the base of her neck, massaging lightly.

"I want no space between us." Her words were urgent. "Zero."

Before she finished, he had her in his lap, her legs straddling his thighs. He gripped her hips, pulling her to him where he needed her most. Through the thin cotton of her leggings, he could feel her warmth.

She gasped while he groaned at how good it felt to have her there. Still clutching his shirt, she twisted the fabric a little, grip tightening.

"What else?" he pressed, his fingertips straying under her sweater just enough to feel silky bare skin above the waistband of her tights.

Her head tipped closer as she gazed down at him, her hair falling forward to frame her face.

"I might need my sweater off for the next part—" she began, only to have her words lost in the muffling of cable knit as he dragged it up her body and off.

High, round breasts wrapped in peach-colored lace were the sexiest thing he'd ever seen.

"Please say you want my mouth here." He canted toward her, breathing the words through the lace so he could see the nipples strain against the fabric.

She arched in answer. "Yes. Kiss me there."

Colt took the request seriously, learning the shape of her with his tongue, teasing her through the material until the lace was wet enough not to matter. Then he peeled it away from her to kiss and lick each breast in turn, his hands returning to her hips so he could keep her fitted against him.

The damp heat of her through the leggings was enough to make him lose it if he let himself go, but he had every intention of seeing this list of hers through to the end.

"Now what, Sierra?" he asked once her hips rode him in an unrelenting rhythm, her fingers now tunneled under his shirt to clutch his bare shoulders.

Her nails lightly scored him with a sting he relished if only to keep him from stripping her naked right here in the middle of the living room.

She paused the rocking to catch her breath, her teeth sinking into her lower lip for a long moment before she spoke again.

"Now take me upstairs and make me forget my own name."

Eight

Colt didn't presume. He didn't press. But once given the green light, he delivered everything Sierra longed for and more.

Already, they were upstairs in the master suite, and she hardly remembered how it had happened with him kissing her the whole way, his hands roaming her body. He'd brought the nursery monitor with him though, the device stowed safely in the back pocket of his jeans.

Heat stole through her middle, a blaze that he stoked higher with every touch, every glide of his tongue over hers. He broke away only to close the door behind them and settle the nursery monitor on the nightstand, while she tried to gain her bearings.

Her gaze darted around the renovated main suite with soothing gray paint except for the one accent wall in reclaimed shiplap behind the quilted headboard of a king-size bed. The dark plank floors and cathedral ceiling kept the focus on the bed, everything else in the room receding compared to that simple focal point with its cream-colored duvet and rows of down pillows. The scents of pine and cedar hung in the air, as if the room were more recently revamped, lit by a single sconce near the entrance to an attached bath.

And then Colt returned, hands wrapping around her waist, lifting her against him so he could resume the drugging kiss. Their bodies meshed, lips molding until she moaned against him, desperate for more.

This time, when he edged back, he didn't release her. He looked into her eyes, his lips brushing hers as he spoke. "I can't believe you're here with me after how many nights I've dreamed of you in this bed."

Pleasure curled through her like a teasing caress.

"We must be having the same dreams." She remembered vividly how many times she'd awoken with an ache that had Colt's name all over it. "Because I've been one room over thinking the same thing."

She reached between them, fidgeting with one of his shirt buttons in an effort to free it. A job he took over with smooth efficiency.

"How am I doing on that list of yours?" He made

quick work of the buttons, momentarily robbing her of speech as he revealed his chest.

Oh. Wow.

Muscles rippled in his shoulders and arms. Ridges created shadows in his abs. Sierra didn't think she could ever look her fill, his body calling to her fingertips to touch and stroke. Trace and lick.

"I'm ready for you to go off script." Light-headed at the promise of what awaited her, she reached for his shoulders to steady herself. "It's been so long for me, I'm not sure I remember what to ask for next."

Even in the dim light of the room, she could see his eyes go a shade darker, the pupils widening.

"Then you can trust I'm going to do everything in my power to give you what you need." His hands skimmed under her sweater to band around her waist, the warmth of his fingers sending a jolt of desire to places that hadn't known a man's touch in years.

She raked her palms down his bare chest, wanting to feel more of him.

"I do trust you," she whispered, surprised to realize how true it was. And it was a trust that extended beyond the bedroom.

She recognized his sense of honor. His need to follow a moral code.

Perhaps he heard the feeling in her voice, the emotion she hadn't intended to show, because his gaze locked with hers for a long moment. But she wasn't ready to examine the emotions stirring inside her. The heat was safer. She lifted higher on her toes to kiss him again, letting her fingers drag lower on his abs until they reached his jeans.

His skin was hot beneath the clothes, her knuckles grazing along the flexing play of muscle. She unfastened the top button and slowly lowered the zipper, careful of the erection straining the denim.

"Sierra." He growled the word in her ear, his hand clamping over hers. Stilling her.

"Mmm?" She swayed against him, hips pressing nearer, pinning their hands between them.

"It's been quite a while for me, too. So this first time might be more of a wild ride."

"First time? I like knowing there will be more than one." She kissed her way along his bristled jaw while she shoved his unbuttoned shirt off his shoulders. "We can call this a practice round."

"I think it's going to feel a whole lot better than practice."

His blue gaze dipped to her breasts spilling out of her peach lace bra, the tight points aching even more under his scrutiny. Unable to wait any longer, she reached for the fastening to remove it, but he caught her fingers to take over the task.

"Let me." He nudged one strap off her shoulder before leaning closer to kiss the place he'd bared. "I want to unwrap you."

She could hardly argue with that. Especially with

the way his mouth descended to her nipple, raising gooseflesh in his wake and sending ribbons of pleasure through her nerve endings. She was used to being in control. To asserting herself to get what she wanted in life.

But maybe right now, with Colt, she could relinquish that need. Surrender to a pleasure he seemed intent on giving her.

Sighing into his kiss, she let her body go limp, certain he would hold her. A thrill went through her as his arms banded tighter around her, lifting her up before settling her in the middle of the massive bed.

She kept her eyes on him, mesmerized by the way he moved over her, shoulders flexing, arms bracketed to keep his weight off her. Only his lips touched her, returning to her breasts. Then his tongue. Then his teeth, dragging the lacy bra cup lower.

Need for him sizzled through her. She arched her back, pressing against him. He answered her by hooking a finger in the waistband of her leggings, hauling them down and off her legs, taking her peach lace panties with them.

She hadn't been naked with anyone in so long. For an instant, she felt a pang of self-consciousness, an awareness of her every imperfection. But the way his hot gaze roamed over her soothed away any concern and brought her back to the moment.

Stroking along his shoulders, she wound her fingers into the hair at his neck and whispered, "I'm ready for my wild ride now."

"You said you were going to trust me." He slid a hand between her knees, one palm spanning her thigh as he edged higher.

The touch robbed her of speech, all her focus on the breath-stealing caress while her heart raced. She clenched his shoulders, steadying herself against the onslaught of sensation when he reached the apex of her thighs and slid a finger over the slick heat there.

"Colt, please," she murmured, her eyes clamping shut to concentrate on the way he made her feel. The way he circled and pressed, stroked and teased her sex.

Her legs were already shaking when he kneed them further apart, planting a kiss where she needed him most. His tongue found the tight, hungry center of her and flicked back and forth, calling forth an orgasm that unraveled her.

Wave after wave of sweetness pummeled her, the pleasure so thick she thought she'd drown in it. By the time the contractions slowed, she felt lightheaded. Thoroughly sated and yet very ready for more at the same time. She blinked her eyes open, wanting to articulate how good she felt.

But Colt was already rolling a condom into place, knowing what they both needed. She arched up off the bed, wrapping her arms around him and holding him close while his heart thundered against her ear.

The sound reminded her that he'd been generous with her pleasure. She longed to return the favor. To make him feel as good as she did.

Wrapping her hand around his rigid length, she stared up into his eyes. "Now it's your turn to trust me."

Colt was hanging by a string.

His every protective, possessive impulse urged him to make Sierra feel good all over again. To ensure she reached that pinnacle of pleasure once more, this time with him inside her.

But with those liquid green eyes fixed on him, and her fingers gliding up and down his shaft in a rhythm that damn near had his eyes crossing, he could deny her nothing.

Not trusting himself to speak, he answered her by rolling her on top of him. She straddled him, her hair falling forward while she stroked him through the condom. He'd never been so glad for an extra layer there since he wasn't sure he could have withstood those silky touches and her fascinated gaze on him otherwise. Not when he hadn't been with another woman since Arielle over a year ago.

He was grateful as hell when she guided him between her legs. He braced himself for the slick heat, but that wasn't enough to prepare him for how good she felt. How right.

A groan tore from his throat, raw and hungry.

He lifted his hips, unable to stop himself from sliding deeper. Sierra's soft gasp filled his ears, and he stroked her hips, steadying her. Hell, maybe it was him that needed steadying. She looked so beautiful, her hair tousled and a little wild from his fingers, her cheeks flushed pink, and bee-stung lips swollen from his kiss. The sight of her made him want to wrap her in his arms for days. Keep her in his bed. Pleasure her so thoroughly she never wanted to leave.

Never? His brain whispered the word back at him. Questioning.

He sank his fingers deeper into the soft curve of her ass, needing to shut out the query he wasn't ready for.

When she began to move again, a slow and gentle rocking of her hips, Colt was all too glad to lose himself in her. He liked the way she gave herself up to the moment, her hands pressing into his skin, imprinting herself on him somehow.

She leaned over him, her blond hair tickling against his collarbone as she kissed his cheek toward his ear. "Get ready. I'm taking my wild ride now."

He didn't have time to chuckle over her impatience or the determined way she approached sex. Because a moment later, her hips bounced and rolled, swayed and bucked. Fireworks blasted across the backs of his eyelids, the feel of her too good for praise. Sweat heated along his shoulders, an inferno building inside him as she moved.

At the last second, he remembered that he should touch her, that he wanted to bring her to that sensual peak once more tonight. Reaching between them, he found the swollen nub he sought and plucked it gently, a movement that had her back arching and her lips gasping his name.

Damn, but he liked how that sounded. Liked the way she spasmed against him so quickly, as if his touch overwhelmed her the same way hers did him.

With her feminine muscles squeezing him tightly, Colt didn't stand a chance of lasting another minute. He gave himself over to the exquisite pressure of her body teasing his, and he was lost to the rush of his own release.

His hoarse shout echoed in the room, his arms banding around her to keep her close while he found completion.

Holy. Hell.

The lush feel of her body had him lost for long minutes. When at last the spasms came to an end, he pulled her down to the bed to lie beside him. He stroked her hair. Kissed her temple. Wondered how to recover from something that felt earth-shattering.

He told himself that was just the side effect of incredible sex. But he wasn't sure he bought it, because he couldn't remember ever feeling this way before. Like he wanted a commitment from her to repeat the experience every night for the rest of time.

Had to be the endorphins, right?

Beside him, Sierra blew a blond strand out of her eyes. "If that was practice, I'm not sure I'm ready for the real thing."

A smile tugged at the corner of his lips. He should be grateful to her for keeping things light.

"I'll take that as a personal challenge. Wait until I get some food in me."

Laughing, she shook her head. "That definitely wasn't meant as a challenge. It might take twenty-four hours for my toes to uncurl."

The warmth that bloomed in his chest felt like more than the effects of a sweet compliment. But damn it, that must be the endorphins, too.

He scrubbed a hand through his hair, wondering how to navigate his next steps without wading any deeper into a relationship that he wasn't ready for. He hadn't thought things through long enough to consider the aftermath of intimacy.

But then the nursery monitor crackled to life. First with the sounds of Micah's restless shifting.

Then with a full-blown, ear-splitting wail.

"I'll get him," Colt assured her, knowing she'd already had a long day with the baby.

Levering himself off the mattress, he found his boxers and dragged them on with a T-shirt before bolting for the nursery to check on his son.

And while he wanted to believe his haste was spurred by being a good father, Colt knew in the back of his mind that his rush wasn't just about running to his son. Without question, he was running from Sierra and the line they'd crossed tonight.

Sierra told herself not to take it personally.

After all, how many new mothers would love to have a partner who sprinted to care for their child at the baby's first cry? Not that she was even the mother of the infant in this case.

And maybe the fact that her brain went there, inserting herself into this household in a maternal capacity, was the only fact she should be concerned with here. Because no matter how much she told herself she was doing a good thing to help Colt bond with Micah—and vice versa—maybe what she was really doing was breaking her own heart. She got more attached to Micah with each passing day. And now she feared she was getting attached to Colt, too.

Sliding out of the big bed in the main suite, she searched for her clothes to make her retreat. She didn't know what was next for her and Colt after what had happened tonight, but the situation required serious thought and reflection. It made no difference that Colt couldn't leave fast enough when he'd heard Micah cry, because she didn't want a romantic relationship with Colt in the first place.

She jammed one foot into her leggings and then the other, remembering how much more fun it had been taking them off. Her whole body was over sensitized after being with Colt, so it was no wonder her emotions were prickly, too. Her face tingled with beard abrasion. Her thighs trembled from using muscles that hadn't been tested in years.

The scent of them lingered in the sheets, tempting her to fall back into the bed. See what would happen when he returned. But those were dangerous thoughts. She couldn't let tonight mean anything more than a momentary pleasure.

After refastening her bra, she retrieved her sweater and slipped it back on. Opening the door that led into the hall, she prepared to return to her own room.

Until Colt's voice sounded over the nursery monitor.

"Hey, big guy. Is it your teeth again? Are they giving you trouble?" The gentleness in his tone made Sierra pause on the threshold.

She glanced over at the monitor still switched on where it rested on the nightstand, listening to the rustling noises of Colt moving around the nursery to soothe his son.

Micah let out another wail that clutched at her heart, making her wonder if she should go help, or at least offer moral support. After her long day of caring for the boy, she knew how exhausting it could be to cope with teething pain.

"I know, little man," Colt continued, his footsteps sounding as he crossed the floor. "It's no fun. Maybe we should check out that teething ring Sierra left in the refrigerator and see if it helps."

The tender, patient way he spoke to his son through the boy's crying was enough to melt her heart. She forgot that she was eavesdropping on a private moment until she heard the nursery door open just two rooms away. And damn if seeing him there, holding Micah in the dim light of the corridor, the baby's face tracked with tears, didn't override all her best intentions to retreat for the night.

"I can get the teething ring for you," she suggested, keeping her gaze on Colt's face instead of his strong thighs. Mostly. "That way you can keep him in the nursery and maybe rock him a little."

"Are you sure?" Colt strode closer, securing Micah in one arm. "I know you've already put your time in."

She bristled a little at the idea that Micah was only a job to her. He was so much more than that. But maybe she shouldn't think that way if Colt was going to take his son to France one day soon, leaving her alone.

"I'll sleep better knowing Micah isn't hurting," she replied a bit stiffly. "It's no trouble."

With that, she spun on her heel and headed for the stairs. If Colt said anything else, she didn't hear it in her rush to retrieve the teether. Was she crazy to have taken this job where she was bound to fall for a dark-eyed baby boy that wasn't hers? Even crazier to let herself get close to the child's compelling father?

Yes. And double yes.

In the kitchen, she made quick work of finding the blue silicone toy in the stainless steel refrigerator. Padding across the hardwood floor in her bare feet, she told herself she would simply pass over the ring and go to bed for the night.

Try to put the intimacy behind her and start fresh in the morning. Focus on her search for the diary around Fenwick Ranch.

Yet as she climbed the stairs to the nursery, Sierra found the idea didn't fill her with the same old enthusiasm it had in the past. As much as she wanted to tell Violetta's story, she wondered how the other woman had done it. How had she parted with her own child to be raised by someone else, just so she could continue to live as Vincent Fenwick, forsaking marriage and motherhood to carve out a successful ranch and a life on her own terms?

Maybe if she found Violetta's diary, she would have the answer. She needed the answer. Because as Sierra walked into the nursery to see Colt and Micah settled in the wooden rocking chair, the baby clutching his toes in one hand while his dark eyes gazed up at his daddy, she couldn't imagine walking away from a life like this. Violetta had done it even though her child had her DNA.

Sierra, on the other hand, had no biological tie to the sweet child in Colt's arms. Yet walking away from Micah would feel like having her heart removed.

To say nothing of Colt.

"Here you go," she said softly, passing over the teething toy and then backing toward the door. "Call me if you have any trouble getting him back to sleep."

He glanced up at her, a flash of something in his blue eyes before he masked it. "I'm sure we'll be fine. And thank you."

Once more, she keenly felt her position as a hired helper.

A temporary nanny, and no more.

Swallowing down a disappointment she had no business feeling, she forced her steps toward the door, not even pausing to wish him a good night. Tomorrow, she'd return to her search for the diary while she watched Micah so that by the time Colt replaced her with a new nanny, Sierra would have the information she needed for her book.

She just wished the task that once excited her professionally didn't feel so damned hollow now.

Nine

The next day, Colt walked a pasture perimeter between the Fenwick place and Black Ranch, looking for a break in the fence. A neighbor had phoned him about a Red Angus cow bearing the Black Ranch brand found wandering around his property, and Colt had sent one of the ranch hands to retrieve the runaway heifer while Colt started the search for a weak spot in the split rail barrier.

The weather was clear and cooler after the intense rains the night before, the fields still damp. Colt appreciated the dose of fresh air after the night with Sierra that had rattled him to the core.

Ducking under a low branch of one of the live oaks that grew along the property line, Colt tugged on a random fence post near a tree root to test its sturdiness.

Still solid. Unlike his personal foundations this morning.

Colt had suspected that he'd said or done the wrong thing when Sierra walked out of the nursery last night, but no matter how many times he reviewed their brief exchanges—both in bed and afterward—he couldn't come up with any idea of what might have offended her. He'd wanted to respond to Micah's cry quickly, knowing she'd had a long day with the baby already. And yet she'd seemed off when she left the nursery.

Too quiet. Hesitant.

Qualities that were completely unlike the Sierra he knew. A far cry from the way she'd been with him in bed. Assertive sometimes and vulnerable others, but he'd never doubted for an instant that she was on board with every single moment they'd shared. Right up until he'd left to check on Micah.

What had happened then? Had the time he'd been gone been enough for her to have cold feet? Morning-after regrets hours ahead of schedule?

Nearing the end of the fence line, Colt paused to lift his Stetson and swipe his hand along his forehead, allowing the cool spring breeze beneath the brim. He approached an old pole barn no longer in use on the Fenwick side of the property line, only

to slow his step when he heard Sierra's voice lifted
in song coming from the opposite side of the barn.

What was she doing out here on this deserted
end of the Fenwick lands?

"...down came the rain and washed the spider
out." Her tune made him smile in spite of the mixed
messages of the night before. She seemed to take
joy in the time spent with his son, and every time
Colt witnessed the two of them together, he was
more convinced they had a special bond.

He envied her ease with the boy, probably because it reminded him that she'd been with Micah
for most of the baby's life while Colt had been un-
aware of the child he'd left behind. The memory of
how he'd failed his son still stung.

Now he paused to listen for a moment before
rounding the building. Micah burst into baby gig-
gles after the spider got washed from the rainspout,
a sure sign Sierra had done something animated to
illustrate the fact.

Then, as she finished her tune, the two of them
laughed softly in unison. And as much as Colt
wanted to simply enjoy the moment, he couldn't
help but remember how much he would be disrupt-
ing Micah and Sierra's bond when he took his son
with him overseas.

Was it a mistake to consider it? Sierra certainly
thought so.

Walking along the side of the brick pole barn

that must have been built about the same time as the original house, Colt turned the corner to see Sierra seated on a hay bale facing Micah, who was still strapped in his stroller. Sierra wore a pair of faded jeans that fit her like a glove, tucked into scuffed cowboy boots. A long pink windbreaker covered her top half, a blond braid resting on one shoulder.

"Good morning," he called as soon as he came into their view, not wishing to startle either of them. "I hear there's a spider problem out here?"

Any doubts that he'd harbored about the mood of their parting last night were only underscored by the troubled expression he glimpsed before she masked it with a polite smile.

"My singing voice is the only trouble we're having," she retorted dryly before turning her attention back to his son. She passed the baby a set of brightly colored toy keys that Micah promptly gummed. "Although Micah is too much of a gentleman to comment on it."

"From what I could hear, he thoroughly enjoyed the performance." He couldn't take his eyes off her, his brain filled with memories of the night before.

Her urgent kisses. Her fingertips moving over him, undressing him. Her orange blossom scent.

Maybe she read his thoughts in his eyes, because she jolted up and off the hay bale to stand. She raised the zipper on her jacket, readying herself to leave.

"I should get Micah back to the house," she announced, swiping bits of hay from her jeans and carefully not meeting his gaze.

"Please don't go on my account." He stepped closer, needing to talk to her. Wanting to set things right.

Or, if nothing else, at least get a better read on what had sent her running in the first place. Last night hadn't been the only time she'd shut down on him inexplicably. There'd been the day they went fishing when she'd dodged his questions. He wouldn't be so quick to back down today.

"I'm not," she insisted, moving to stand behind the stroller, already gripping the handle bar. "Micah and I have a long walk back to the house."

For a moment, he wondered what had brought her all the way out here to the old, unused outbuilding, but he shoved aside the thought in an effort to keep her there.

"Sierra, please. We need to talk." He covered her hand with his. Entreating. "I've been going over last night in my mind, and I'm not sure where things went wrong."

A barn swallow swooped out from under the eaves to sit on an oak tree limb, chirping happily with a big group of them.

Sierra stared after them before turning back to him.

"Nothing went wrong." She slid her hand out from under his and tucked it in the pocket of her windbreaker. "I just got caught up in my thoughts afterward, I guess."

Her teeth caught her lower lip, stopping whatever else she might have said. He recognized the gesture, remembering the way she'd shut down their conversation the last time he'd tried to confront her about something that bothered her.

"All the more reason we should talk about what happened." He glanced down at his son to see Micah happily shaking the plastic keys Sierra had given him, his eyelids drooping. Colt leaned closer to adjust the back of the stroller so the baby reclined more. "Micah looks ready to nod off any second, so we have time."

"But there isn't anything to say." She spread her arms wide, voice frustrated. "We knew going into last night that you're not even planning to stay in Royal and you'll be replacing me soon. I'm temporary in every way for you, and I understand that. It's fine."

His stomach burned with acid to think that was what she'd taken away from their night together. A night that had meant something more to him. Perhaps if he'd been a better communicator with Arielle, he would have known about his son sooner. He needed to learn how to press for answers. How to convey concern without pushing people away.

"It's not fine. And I sure as hell never meant to give you the impression that *you* were temporary— only the nanny position, since I know you have other work commitments." He wished he could read her better, but even after their amazing night together, he still couldn't gauge her. "Just because I have business overseas—"

"Business important enough to bring Micah. Indefinitely." She folded her arms, her chin lifting. "Don't minimize it."

"Okay. Just because I have obligations to the winery doesn't mean you're a temporary part of my life. Or Micah's." Although he knew from her expression that sounded hypocritical when he'd told her weeks ago that he didn't want to get involved for that very reason. "Last night took us by surprise. We haven't had time to figure out what it means or what happens next. But we *should*."

She shook her head, blond hair swishing softly against the pink windbreaker. "Last night didn't change anything. I know that, and so do you. I'm not looking for a relationship any more than you are. You're focused on Micah. I need to focus on my book."

He wanted to argue with her, not liking the vision of himself as someone who indulged personal desires in a way that could hurt others. But hadn't he done just that? Not only with Sierra, but with Arielle, too? Except, damn it, no matter how much he screwed things up with this lovely, strong, determined woman, he wouldn't risk the bond she shared with his son.

He paced away from her, trying to pull his thoughts together so he didn't alienate her further.

"First of all, you're not a temporary part of Micah's life if you don't want to be." Turning on his heel, he faced her again in time to see her lower the shade on the stroller to shield more of Micah from the sun. "You're so good to him. And it's obvious he adores you. I want him to be happy."

She blinked fast, not looking at him. When she spoke, her voice sounded thin. Thready. "Thank you."

Something was obviously wrong. Something he still wasn't understanding. He moved closer to her as she bent to gently pry the toy keys out of Micah's hand now that the boy had fallen asleep.

"What is it?" He laid a hand on her shoulder, only to discover she was shaking. "What's the matter?"

"I'm sorry," she sniffed through unshed tears, exhaling a long, unsteady breath. "You know I've gotten attached to Micah, and it's been so fun to be with him." She closed her eyes for a moment before turning toward him. Meeting his gaze. "But occasionally it stirs a personal regret for me since I can't have children of my own."

Sierra had never shared that with another soul.

Not even her adopted mother knew the secret pain she carried, the reason she hadn't dated in years. Sierra had always thought it better to lock down her condition and not speak about it, refusing to be damaged goods in anyone's eyes.

Yet no matter how carefully she guarded her prognosis, protecting herself from anyone else's unwanted opinions or sympathy, she couldn't change the fact that she *felt* damaged.

Logically, she knew that was ridiculously unfair to herself. She would never view someone else as lacking because of a medical condition. The very idea was abhorrent to her. And yet, deep inside, logic didn't apply to her sense of self, where she still felt the lack of normal biological function like a giant void. The loss of her dreams for a husband and family one day.

She thought all of that in the moment after her confession. In that smallest slice of time where Colt processed her words.

To his credit, she saw only concern and empathy in his blue eyes in the moment before he wrapped her in his arms.

"Honey, I'm so damned sorry." He spoke the words against her hair while he hugged her tight, his hands rubbing over her back in a way that really did comfort her.

A soft sob bubbled free, but it was more a cry of relief to have shared the burden. She hadn't realized how much weight she'd given it by keeping it locked inside for so long.

"Thank you." She burrowed deeper into his shoulder, grateful for his warmth. His strength. His compassion that didn't feel like pity. "I'm not normally such a mess about it. I thought I'd made peace with it—"

She cut herself off, knowing how far from the truth that was. She'd done some counseling that her doctor had recommended after her diagnosis, but the therapist had warned her the emotional toll of infertility could return in a myriad of ways throughout her life. Just because she'd found a way to cope these last few years didn't mean the ache was gone.

He kissed the top of her head, still stroking his hands along her back. "Thank you for telling me. For trusting me with that."

She closed her eyes for a long moment, still soaking up the feel of him. The scent of pine and sandalwood closed around her, the canvas of his jacket enveloping her along with his arms. But then, remembering that she was trying to resurrect boundaries after their night together, she forced herself to straighten.

"I appreciate you listening without judgment." She swiped her hand across her eyes before tipping her head back to look up into the tree full of tiny chirping birds. "Half the reason I've never told anyone about the infertility is a fear that someone will try and cheer me up about it with a platitude or offer advice."

She'd heard stories like that in one of the counseling group sessions. Exhausted women on their third round of IVF would confide that "well-meaning" friends told them it would help if they "relaxed more" during sex. Sierra knew herself well enough to know she ran the risk of decking someone who made a comment like that to her, so in the interest of all parties, she'd never shared the truth.

"You've never told anyone?" Colt repeated her words back to her, making her aware she'd unwittingly revealed even more than she'd planned.

Making her aware how much she'd come to trust him in spite of herself. How much she genuinely liked him as a person, above and beyond the physical attraction. Dragging in a deep breath, she turned to face him again.

His Stetson cast his face half in shadow, but she felt the intensity of that blue gaze just the same.

"It's very personal," she explained, not wanting to dwell on the whys and wherefores when she'd already shared too much. "I've never had cause to tell anyone else—outside of a counseling group. But I thought it only fair that you know since I occasionally wrestle with the emotional aspects of infertility. Like when I play with Micah or—like last week—when I hear you talk about what makes a good mother. Even when the mother in question is a cow."

She managed a wry smile at the admission, recognizing how sensitive it sounded.

Colt didn't smile though. He shook his head, blowing out a frustrated breath as he scraped a hand along his jaw. "I wish I'd known. I don't remember what I said, but I have no business passing judgment on what makes for a good parent. I do know you've been here for Micah when I haven't been, and that makes you far better equipped than me to be a caregiver."

His heartfelt words slid right past the barriers she'd tried to resurrect this morning. A tenderness welled inside her for his kindness. His recognition that she had good maternal instincts even though the baby she'd cared for wasn't her own.

Perhaps that shouldn't mean so much to her. Yet considering he was Micah's father, the man she'd searched for relentlessly for months, she hugged the words close and let them be a balm for the ragged parts of her soul.

But she knew that was all they could ever be. No matter how nice it felt to have Colt's acknowledgment of her role in Micah's life, she had to steel herself for losing them both soon. And maybe that was for the best since she'd given up on the idea of a family long ago. She shouldn't let herself get lulled into the idea that she could be a part of Colt's life.

"Thank you, Colt." She moved toward the stroller, knowing she needed to make a fast exit.

Her feelings were too all over the place. Too close to the surface. "That means a lot to me."

"I can drive you and Micah back to the house," he offered, scuffing a boot through the dried straw on the ground outside the pole barn. "My truck is about a quarter of a mile back that way."

Gesturing with his thumb, he indicated the opposite direction of the Fenwick homestead.

"That's all right." She didn't dare spend any more time alone with him. It was too risky when she remembered how good it felt to be in his arms. "My walks with Micah are my main source of exercise lately, and it's gorgeous out today."

His brow furrowed, and she knew that he debated pressing the issue. But thankfully, he only nodded.

"All right. Don't forget we have two nanny candidates interviewing this evening. I'm hoping you and Micah will be there to help me decide." He withdrew his phone from the back pocket of his jeans, the screen alight as it buzzed. "Sorry. This is my winery office in Cahors."

"Of course, please do take it." She welcomed the opportunity for escape, needing to collect herself and her thoughts before the nanny interviews that would put her one step closer to being out of Micah's life.

And Colt's.

"Wait, Sierra." Colt held up a hand to stop her, swiping aside the incoming call in a way that made the device quit vibrating. "I can call them back later." Returning the phone to his pocket, he continued, "I just wanted to make sure they're shipping over some Royal Black wines for the local Wine and Roses Festival. But I'm more interested in knowing what made you two come out to the pole barn? It's a rough walk with the stroller."

Her heart pounded harder at the question, knowing she needed to talk to Colt about her search for Violetta Ford's diary. Would he think it a fool's errand? Or would he somehow see her interest in Violetta as undermining her caregiving role for Micah?

She'd like to think he knew her better than that. But she couldn't forget how quickly he'd dismissed her journalism efforts when they'd first met.

I figured you were just digging for an inside track on the Texas Cattleman's Club for one of your stories... His words echoed in her head now.

"Just looking for new sights to see," she told him. A half truth, certainly. But she'd shared enough for one day. "How about you? What are you doing out this way?"

"A cow broke out of this pasture last night during the storm. I'm trying to find where she got through the fence." He gestured toward the Black Ranch side of the split rails.

Guilt pinched that she hadn't told him the real reason she was surveying the Fenwick property. But she would have time enough once she narrowed her search. Or found the diary.

"Good luck, then." Tucking her hair behind one ear, she turned to leave him, pushing the stroller over the dirt path that was definitely a bit lumpy. Especially after the rain. "I'll see you for the interviews later," she called over her shoulder.

Colt lifted a hand to wave, and she hurried away. Too bad her guilty conscience kept her company the whole way home.

Ten

Seated at the dining room table that evening, Colt stared unseeing at the printed résumé in front of him. The young woman currently interviewing for the position of Micah's nanny seemed supremely qualified on paper. That didn't mean Colt wanted to hire her.

How could he even consider replacing Sierra?

His fingers flexed underneath the table while Sierra exchanged small talk with the woman. Katie? Kaitlyn? It didn't matter since he didn't want to employ this candidate or the other one they'd met with over the course of the evening.

Because while—he focused on the résumé paper until the name came into view—Katie-Lynn might be accomplished enough to bathe, feed and care for a six-month-old, she sure as hell could never take the place of Sierra Morgan.

Micah loved Sierra.

As for Colt? He didn't know how to label the relationship he shared with Sierra, especially after their night together. But he appreciated how happy she made his son, and he respected that she'd been relentless in her search for Colt after Micah had been left orphaned. Now that he was aware of her personal journey with infertility, her selflessness with regard to Micah seemed all the more admirable. How tough must it be for her to get close to the boy, knowing Colt would take him overseas soon?

Frustration kicked harder.

"Thank you for stopping by," Colt announced abruptly, coming to his feet to call an end to the interview.

The startled expression on Sierra's face, though fleeting, told him he'd been rude. But then, he hadn't really been listening to the exchange in the first place. Damn it.

Still, Sierra covered for him, assuring Katie-Lynn they'd be in touch with all of the candidates within the next few days and thanking her again with more warmth than Colt had managed. Both women took a moment to admire Micah in his deluxe baby swing, banging the tray with a toy rattle while his happy grin showed off two tiny bottom teeth.

As soon as the young woman was out the door, however, Sierra spun on Colt.

"What was that all about?" Hands on hips, she glared at him. "If you want a good relationship with a new nanny, you shouldn't begin it by chasing her off. I thought she seemed ideal."

"She's far from ideal," he retorted, brushing past her to wind the baby swing. Then, lowering himself until he was eye level with his son, he tickled the boy's toes through mint-green footie pajamas.

Micah kicked gleefully and tossed the rattle in his excitement. The kid couldn't be any cuter. And he deserved better than just some random job applicant with a background in early childhood education.

"Care to share what you could have possibly found lacking in her?" Sierra asked, retrieving the rattle and laying it on the coffee table instead of passing it back to Micah.

Colt had noticed how diligent she was about washing toys that the baby dropped before returning them to him. One of a million ways she took care of Micah better than someone else might. Did Katie-Lynn know Micah's favorite nursery rhymes or how quickly the boy could kick off a pair of socks if they weren't a special brand?

"She's just not the right person." Standing, he

faced her, knowing he didn't have a good reason for the stubborn stance. "It's not about what's on a résumé. It's a gut feeling that I have about her." He extended his arms wide, a gesture of surrender. "Whether it makes sense or not, I'm going to follow my instincts. Micah's my son, and I only just found him, so I'm not trusting his care with just anyone."

Her shoulders sagged, hands falling away from her narrow hips.

"You're right." She nodded, her blond pony-tail swinging as she moved around the living area, tidying a few papers and toys that had ended up strewn around the room during the interview sessions. "You have to feel one hundred percent at ease with whoever you hire to care for your son."

Was he right? He almost regretted that she'd agreed so readily, his unsettled nerves all too prepared to argue the point, even if he didn't fully understand the reasons.

Because he needed to supplant Sierra in the first place? Because Colt would be returning to France as soon as Micah seemed more comfortable with him? Damned if he knew.

"You're better with him than anyone else," he found himself saying, his attention remaining fixed on the swing, where Micah's head tipped to one side of the blue padded seat. It was easier than wrestling with his feelings for the woman in front of him, her green eyes seeing too much. "I'm trying not to infringe on your time any more than I already have. But is there any way you can continue helping out with him until I'm ready to—"

She made a soft sound, a hum of protest maybe. Or resignation?

"Colt. Don't ask me to do that." Her voice cracked. "You know I'm very attached to him already. The more time I spend with him, the harder it's going to be to say goodbye when you leave."

Emotion lay heavy in her tone, and he whipped around to see her face. Gauge her expression. Was it only Micah who would tug at her heart when he left? Or would she miss him sometimes, too?

Even as he thought it, however, he dismissed the idea. She'd been very clear about not wanting a relationship. And from the way she'd drawn boundaries between them, he believed her. Besides, who could blame her for feeling a special tenderness toward Micah after what she'd confided in Colt today?

He berated himself for being ten kinds of selfish bastard for thinking about himself after what Sierra had shared with him earlier. Of course she was only thinking of Micah.

"I have no right to ask anything more from you," he agreed, recognizing that he needed to buck up and hire someone else so that Sierra could establish whatever relationship she felt most comfortable having with Micah. Perhaps it would be easier for her to separate a little at a time. "You've been far more generous to me than I've deserved, and I appreciate how much of your personal time you've devoted to Micah. And me, too."

She lifted a brow at him. Indignant. "I wasn't on the clock with you."

He shook his head with impatience. "I don't mean that, obviously. But you've taken time to teach me how to be a better father. You didn't have to explain childcare to me as you tended Micah, but you always do." He recalled how she'd helped him shop online for toys that would help with the boy's coordination, not just items that were cute. And whenever she discovered things Micah liked, games or songs or a new twist on a bedtime ritual, she shared the discovery with Colt. "I'm more confident with him now because of that."

"Oh. You've done plenty of kindnesses for me, too." She shifted her weight from foot to foot, seeming uneasy. "I've appreciated the chance to stay here. My room at the B and B was beginning to feel a little claustrophobic after a five-month residency. So you've more than paid me back for anything I've taught you about babies."

For a moment, they locked eyes in the room gone quiet except for the ticking of the swing as the motion slowed down again. Sierra glanced away first, her cheeks slightly pink as she looked down at the baby. Micah had fallen asleep, his Cupid's bow mouth blowing a tiny, drooly bubble as he exhaled.

"Where will you go——" Colt began, not sure how to frame the question in a way that wouldn't set them at odds again. "If I hire someone to take your place? Back to the Cimarron Rose?"

"Most likely." She'd changed into a black knit dress for the interviews, the outfit both more formal and subdued than her usual clothes. The simple lines outlined her trim curves without drawing attention to itself.

Yet Colt found it difficult to look away from her.

"How much longer do you think you'll stay in Royal to research the book on Violetta and the Texas Cattleman's Club?" He regretted not asking her more about the project before now, but he'd had his hands full with figuring out fatherhood.

Not to mention the efforts he'd put into checking on Black Ranch, overseeing renovations on the Fenwick house, and making preparations for the Royal Black Winery to participate in the Wine and Roses Festival at the end of the month. The fact that a local wine event existed in Royal in the first place had got him thinking about the possibility of one day opening a local branch of the Royal Black brand. There were plenty of Central Texas wineries that had met with success.

"It's difficult to say." She ran a hand along her ponytail, settling it along her shoulder in a way that stirred her fragrance. "I'm still tracking source material," she said vaguely before bending toward the swing. "I should put Micah to bed."

Had the question made her uncomfortable? Or was their proximity stirring awareness for her the way it did for him?

"Please. Allow me to take over the task tonight." Colt's hand landed on the small of her back, the warmth of her skin evident through the knit dress.

He told himself to move his hand away from her, but his fingers only flexed and clenched against the soft fabric while he struggled with the need to touch more of her.

Straightening, Sierra's green eyes flashed to his. Awareness pinged between them like an electric charge, buzzing up his arm. Settling in his gut.

But before he could act on it, her expression shuttered again, and she darted away.

"Thank you, Colt. I'm grateful for the extra time to work." Pausing beside an end table, she scooped up her tablet and a legal pad with some notes on it. "Good night."

Of all the lies that Sierra had told herself in the weeks since she'd met Colt Black, the most egregious was that she would *work* tonight when all she could think of was the way his blue eyes had burned into her earlier.

The way his broad palm had spanned her back,

the fingers raking lightly against the material of her dress.

Two hours later, she sat alone in the recently re-modeled upstairs den, staring blankly at the screen of her tablet while she remembered snippets from the night she'd spent in Colt's bed. How quickly his brief touch tonight had stirred those memories.

The way he'd kissed her as if he couldn't get enough. The way he'd teased a response from her long slumbering libido, awakening hungers she'd believed she had conquered.

How was she going to resurrect the boundary between them when his touch was so magnetic? When the man himself compelled her like no one else?

The diary, she reminded herself harshly, straightening in one of the low barrel chairs to refocus on the tablet in her lap. Work had always been her way to keep herself from thinking about her old dreams of a family, and she would trust that it could be all-absorbing once again if she allowed herself to get immersed in it.

"If I were Violetta," she asked herself aloud, using two fingers to expand the map of the Fenwick property currently on her screen, "where would I hide a diary?"

She'd searched most of the outbuildings already, including the pole barn where she'd run into Colt. The only structures left to search were the old cellar underneath the house itself—a task she'd put off since the work crew in charge of renovations frequently passed through the basement—and a couple of ruins on the property that hadn't been cleared. One was the remnants of an old windmill with a limestone base, the other a fallen chicken coop.

Tomorrow, she'd tackle at least one of those spots. The cellar might have to wait until the weekend when the work crew took a day off. For now, she enlarged a photo of the windmill, turning the screen this way and that to see if she could find a likely place to start looking. She couldn't dig up the whole property, but she might bring a shovel to explore likely areas. Sierra assumed that Violetta would have tried to hide her diary somewhere that would be protected from too much water or sun. Somewhere safe from paper-loving rodents.

Tapping the screen twice, she brought up a different angle of the windmill, noting a few crevices in the remaining limestone. Could a diary fit in one of them?

She felt some of the old enthusiasm for the project returning. Violetta Ford really was an interesting character with her refusal to accept the proscribed outlines of what a woman's life was supposed to be. She'd lived on her own terms.

Not even a baby had slowed Violetta down. She'd ensured the child was raised by his dad. Dean was the one who could take the best care of him.

Had that been Sierra's mother's thinking when

she'd left Sierra on the church doorstep? Someone better suited for caring? She hoped so.

Thoughtfully, Sierra switched off the tablet and stood, the baby thoughts reminding her she hadn't gone in to kiss Micah good-night. Not that the little boy would know since Colt had put him to sleep hours ago.

But she could hover over his crib for a moment and enjoy the sight of his sweet face in slumber before she sought her own bed. Once Colt hired another nanny, she wouldn't be able to share this ritual with the baby anymore.

Quietly, she left the den and walked down the hallway toward the nursery, pushing open the door already left slightly ajar. She didn't want to wake Micah, of course. But she also didn't want Colt to hear her on the other end of the baby monitor.

Moonlight streamed in through one of the partially closed blinds, the dull blue beams enough to illuminate the room she knew well by now with its sky-blue walls and cherrywood furnishings. The scent of the baby's laundry detergent and shampoo stirred in the slowly turning ceiling fan. As she stepped deeper into the room, her gaze went to the crib tucked in the far corner.

Only to spot the tall, imposing shadow of Colt leaning over the side rail.

Her breath caught in her throat, and she stifled a gasp of surprise to see him there. One elbow leaned on the cherrywood crib rail while, with his other hand, he stroked the dark, wispy curls off his son's forehead.

And then it wasn't just a gasp but a sudden lump in her throat at the tender display, especially coming from a man who'd struck her as coolly serious. Reserved. She'd tried so hard to keep some distance between them since their night together. To keep in perspective that what they'd shared wouldn't last. Yet seeing him here, now, stirred all of her feelings for him, never far from the surface.

Biting her lip, she stood motionless in the center of the room, hating to interrupt the moment. But before she could decide what to do next, Colt's voice rasped softly.

"I know you think it's a mistake for me to leave Royal with him." His words weren't at all what she'd expected. He didn't look up at her as he continued to smooth his fingers through the child's hair. "But it seems more important than ever that I provide him the best possible legacy. He deserves that. It doesn't mean I'm cutting him off from his mom's side. His aunt Eve will always have a place in his life, as will Cammie, and you."

Still she hesitated, feeling like an interloper at a private, family time. Or maybe she was just more sensitive to it because she'd been so careful not to let herself feel like a part of this family. Even when the temptation weighed heavily on her.

And yet, Colt deserved an answer. Clearly, he'd put a lot of thought into carving out a future for his son.

"It's only natural to want to do everything in the world for your child." She closed the distance between them, drawn to the spot beside Colt near the crib. For the man? Or for the chance to see Micah?

The warmth of Colt's nearness permeated her thin sleep T-shirt and pajama pants, the comfy clothes she'd changed into for working on her book research. She kept her gaze on Micah, knowing the sexy single dad was too much of a draw at any time of day, but especially here, alone, in the dark.

"I never would have guessed how much everything in my world would change in an instant." Colt straightened from the crib, standing at his full height as he shifted to face her. "And in spite of what you think, Sierra, I'm trying to do the right thing for him."

Her pulse quickened as his attention fell fully on her, and her eyes sought his despite the dark. There was enough moonlight for her to see his shadowed jaw, her fingers itching to test the texture of it. She'd liked feeling the slight burn from it on her neck. Her breasts and thighs.

"I know you are," she acknowledged, wishing she didn't sound so breathless and hungry. "But I can't help offering a different perspective for you to consider. Maybe it's too much in my nature to stir things up."

"I'm glad you do." His voice sent a pleasurable shiver up her spine. "You push me to weigh and consider my next move. Now that there's a baby involved, I can't afford to take solely myself into account."

It wasn't the first kind thing he'd said to her today. Earlier, after the nanny interviews, he'd intimated that she was the best person for the job because she loved Micah. Part of her relished the privileged role she had here. Another part of her feared she wouldn't be able to walk away from the draw of the man and his adorable son.

Except what choice would she have when he left?

And what if he accused her of using her position here to further her career ambitions once he discovered she was searching for Violetta's diary? No question, she should tell him about her search for that last missing piece of the woman's life in Royal.

Licking suddenly dry lips, Sierra laid a hand on his arm to begin.

Just as Colt's arms banded around her, his mouth descending on hers in a slow, claiming kiss.

Heat stirred inside her. Like banked coals being flipped and prodded into new life, all the emotions she'd struggled to tamp down now flared to brightness. The attraction to Colt. The love for his child. The private heartbreak she'd tried so hard to ignore these last few years. All the feelings made the kiss that much more potent.

Made her desperate to get lost in it when none of this would last much longer.

Colt was leaving. He'd take Micah with him. A new nanny would get them through their last days before they returned to France. And as for Sierra, it felt like this might be her last chance to explore the big, powerful emotions of a life that would never belong to her.

The life of a mother.

And, she couldn't help imagining for a moment, a cherished wife. Would anyone blame her if she wanted to experience how that dream might have felt for just one more night?

Eleven

Had he read the moment correctly?

Colt had felt the attraction streak through him like a lightning bolt the instant Sierra stepped into the nursery, but he'd forced himself to move slowly, making sure they were on the same page after their awkward parting the night before. Now, with her slender arms twining around his neck and her body pressed tightly to his, he had his answer.

She still wanted him, too.

If her urgent kisses were any indication, she needed him every bit as desperately as he craved her. Even now, her hands tunneled under his shirt, fingers deftly traveling over his abs to trace the waistband of his jeans.

He felt every dip and hollow through the thin sleep shirt she wore. Her breasts molded to his chest, her curves all the softer without the barrier of undergarments. She wore nothing beneath the sleep shirt and cotton pajama pants, the feel of her body making him ready to back her against the nearest door to be inside her.

Except they needed to take this somewhere else. Now.

With an effort, he broke the kiss enough to speak against her lips.

"Let me take you to my bed," he urged, stroking over her shoulders and down her back, pressing her against him.

"Yes, please," she agreed, her slight nod moving her lips up and down against his.

Need thrummed heavier with every beat of his heart, and he wasted no time lifting her against him to carry her where he wanted her. He paused just long enough to grab the baby monitor off a small stand by the rocking chair so they could bring it with them. Then, a moment later, they were out of the nursery and in the hallway that led to the master suite.

Every step he took rocked their bodies together. Every step made his blood burn hotter for this woman who'd gotten so deep under his skin he didn't know how he'd ever dig her out.

Or if he even wanted to.

Inside his room, he tossed the monitor on a dresser and kicked the door shut behind them. And then, he really did back her up against it, giving her another slow, thorough kiss that had them both breathing hard.

Sierra arched against him, her thighs scissoring against one of his while she strained closer. His lifted her higher, guiding her hips more firmly to his. If not for the clothes they still wore, he'd be inside her.

As it was, the heat of her sex branded him through his jeans, the damp warmth evident through the seam of her pajamas.

"Hurry," she murmured against his mouth, the sound of their breathing harsh in the otherwise quiet room. "Please, hurry."

Were they experiencing this over-the-top need because they'd been interrupted the night before? Because they hadn't been able to take their time with one another the way he'd wanted to? Or would it always be like this between them, a hunger that felt like he'd been starving for her?

He couldn't afford to think about that now when she'd made her wishes clear. Releasing her from where he'd pinned her to the door, he carried her in his arms to the edge of the king-size bed. He settled her there long enough for him to retrieve a box of condoms from the nightstand.

And in that minute, she'd already unbuttoned the

lower half of his shirt to sweep aside enough for her
to kiss and lick her way along his abs.

A growl rolled up his throat, but he stifled the
sound, spearing his fingers into her silky hair instead. The gesture must have encouraged her, because she went to work on his fly, opening it enough
to free him.

Then, tugging his cotton boxers lower with one
hand, she wrapped the rigid length of him in the
other, gliding up and down before she bent her head
to kiss and lick him there.

This time, he didn't have a chance in hell of sup-
pressing a growl of pleasure. Of need.

"Sierra." He said her name like a warning, but he
didn't know what from. He only knew he could get
lost in her if he allowed himself. "Tonight, you're
not leaving until after the sun rises."

She peeped up at him through lowered lashes,
green eyes scorching him before she swirled her
tongue around him, driving him clear out of his
mind for her.

"I'll take that as a yes." He tore off his shirt the
rest of the way, then turned his attention to hers,
skimming it up her back and over her shoulders
before he laid her down on the mattress.

Staring up at him, Sierra followed his movements, her cheeks flushed pink and her lips swollen.
He couldn't get enough of her, a surge of posses-
siveness gaining momentum as he skimmed off her

pajama bottoms and made room for himself between her thighs.

But then she cupped his cheek in her hand, her thumb smoothing along his bottom lip, the gesture checking his hunger enough to kiss her thoroughly all over again.

While he lost himself in the give-and-take of her lips and tongue, she palmed a condom and tore it open. Her fingers maneuvered a little awkwardly as she rolled the latex into place, her tentative touch making him feel protective of her even as his hips rocked toward her.

The soft sound she made in response shredded the last of his restraint. Knowing that she wanted this as much as he did urged him on. Had him gripping her hips to guide her where he needed her.

Her fingernails bit lightly into his shoulders as he eased inside her. He welcomed the sting, a counterpoint to how incredible she felt all around him. Looking down into her eyes, he sank deeper. A connection to her sliding into place.

He would have sworn she experienced it, too, because he thought he saw an answering light in her green gaze. The beginnings of something bigger than either of them had planned for. A bond that might weather time apart or even being on different continents.

But then, closing her eyes, Sierra wrapped her legs around his waist. Colt forgot everything but the sensation of her body squeezing his, molding and giving all around him.

Had he dreamed that moment when there'd been something more?

Sierra had never clung to a man before.

Not figuratively. Not even physically.

But she couldn't deny a serious amount of clinging going on right now with Colt. She couldn't let go of him. Couldn't get enough. She needed more. Deeper. Faster.

Or maybe she just told herself that she needed those things. Because for a second she could have sworn she'd looked into Colt's eyes and thought she wanted forever. A tenderness had welled up inside her, so soft and warm that she feared it would swallow her whole. So like a coward, she shut it down fast and concentrated on just this one moment.

The lush completion she felt at being in his arms and in his bed. And oh God, she didn't want to think about how hard it would be to walk away after this night with him. Why had she ever thought it would help to know how good it would feel to live the fantasy that could never be hers?

For now, she locked her ankles behind his hips, keeping him close. The hard planes of his body flexed and shifted, muscles rippling as he worked deeper and then withdrew, creating a rhythm that stole her breath. Made her whimper.

She realized she'd allowed her nails to sink into his shoulders, so she smoothed the crescent moon marks with her fingertips, trying to recover some control of herself. Finding it so much tougher than she'd ever imagined.

With her emotions raw and her body clamoring for more of him, Sierra had never felt so exposed. Like another stroke might shatter her. She couldn't untwine herself from him, though. Couldn't stop herself from following these addictive sensations through to their natural conclusion.

Her breath came faster, heart slamming against her rib cage like it might really break free.

"Colt." She said his name over and over, wearing it out, not caring how lost she sounded. Because right now, she was.

Lost.

And Colt felt like her only anchor.

"Sierra. Look at me," he whispered, voice ragged with his own harsh breathing. He paused his thrusts, going still on top of her as he stared down at her in the moonlight.

She swallowed hard and lifted her lashes, taking in the intensity of his blue eyes turned dark. Only when their gazes locked did he touch her, the pads of his fingers circling the aching bud of her sex before he sank into her again. Slowly.

His touch unraveled her.

An orgasm blindsided her, the release coming

hard and fast as sensations rocked her. Her eyes fell closed again so she could soak in all the delectable ways he made her body feel.

When at last the shuddering subsided, Colt kissed her temple lightly before pushing deeper inside again. The pressure spurred more flutters of her feminine muscles, like a sensual reminder of what he could do to her.

Then he built a new rhythm all over again. Harder. Faster. A rhythm more for him, except that she loved it just as much. She wanted him to feel as incredible as she had. Needed for him to remember this night the way she would. They couldn't have a future together. But they could have a taste of how amazing it might have been if things had been different.

So when at last his thrusts were enough to even make the whole bed shudder, Sierra let them carry her away with him. Her body, already so sensitive from his touches, seized in another orgasm. The release spurred his own a moment later, his hips punching forward one last time to fill her completely. Their groans of completion mingled with their breath, hearts pounding madly.

In the long moments of stillness afterward, there was no sound except for the windy exhales growing more and more quiet. Even that rhythm synched up, until their chests seemed to rise and fall together.

Colt rolled to his side, taking her with him, so

they lay there facing one another in the moonlight fading as the night deepened. She closed her eyes when he stroked her hair from her eyes, not sure she could hide the tenderness she felt.

Knowing neither of them was ready for those emotions.

He was leaving.

She was committed to her work for a good reason.

Sierra breathed the reminders in and out along with her slowed respirations, the mantra she needed to keep her heart in one piece after this night together. Would the affirmations work?

Tucking her head against Colt's chest, she shut down the question and simply hoped for the best. Because she cared about this man deeply. Maybe even loved him. Perhaps that was why she needed for him to be happy, even if it meant being apart.

She'd given up her dreams of family long ago, so she'd never try to tie him to her. But for the first time, she understood that letting him go would cost her far more than she'd ever imagined.

The doorbell rang at noontime the next day, right on schedule for Micah's lunch date. Sierra tightened her ponytail as she hurried to answer it, peeking briefly out the front window to be sure the guests were the ones she'd been expecting. She welcomed the distraction since she wasn't ready to think about the explosive encounter with Colt last night or what it meant.

Haley Lopez was the police officer who'd been the first to respond to the call of Micah being found abandoned in the Royal Memorial Hospital parking lot, and she'd continued to track Micah's story with as much interest as Sierra had. And sure enough, tall, gorgeous Haley stood on the welcome mat, her long dark hair blowing lightly around her face as she leaned into her real estate developer boyfriend, Jackson Michaels.

"Hello!" Sierra greeted them both warmly as she opened the front door, waving them inside. "I'm so glad it worked out for you to visit Micah today."

"I've been dying to see him," Haley enthused, stepping over the threshold as her eyes went straight to the baby blanket on the floor of the living room where Micah was having tummy time. "Oh, look at him! He's grown so much in just the last month."

Haley had messaged her a few times about getting together so she could see Micah, but the timing hadn't worked out until today. Behind Haley, Jackson stepped inside and shut the door behind him, nodding a greeting to Sierra while Haley moved toward the baby.

"Is Colt home?" Jackson asked, glancing around the house. "I see his work crew is doing a nice job on the renovations."

Sierra swallowed a moment's discomfort at the

question since she'd been the tiniest bit relieved when Colt was called away an hour ago.

"Colt couldn't be here. He went to the Texas Cattleman's Club a little while ago," she explained as they followed Haley into the living area. "The coordinator for the Wine and Roses Festival messaged him about a problem with the shipment of Royal Black wines for the event, so he went to help straighten things out."

After she'd assured him she'd be fine on her own for the rest of the day. Yes, their night together had been perfect, and she'd awakened to the scent of breakfast cooking for her. But she wasn't sure how long she could hide how wrecked she felt about their time together coming to an end. If Colt had sensed that she wrestled with morning-after jitters, he hadn't acknowledged it. He'd served her eggs and pancakes as if it were the most natural thing in the world to share the first meal of the day together.

But Sierra had needed a chance to pull herself together after the intensity of the night they'd shared. She knew the longer they continued to see one another, the greater the stakes would be for a breakup. For Micah especially. She needed to get this right.

"Well, we're only too happy to offer some babysitting relief," Haley assured her from her spot on the floor where she already lay across from Micah. She shook the soft bunny rattle, encouraging him to reach for the toy. "Jackson and I can stay for a couple of hours, so whatever you need to do, don't mind us. I'll be in baby heaven playing with this little guy."

Sierra smiled, appreciating how easygoing Haley didn't mind playing on the floor.

"Actually, I do have a few errands outside the house as long as you're here." Sierra shouldn't feel guilty about that, since she'd put in far more hours caring for Micah than duty called for since she hardly viewed her time with the baby as a job.

But given that she wanted to search the windmill for Violetta's diary today, she couldn't help a twinge of conscience since she hadn't spoken to Colt about it yet. She'd only promised not to write any more stories on Micah, so why should he mind about her research into Violetta's past for her book? Yet some instinct warned her he wouldn't be thrilled that she was conducting her search on his property.

In her work as an investigative journalist, she was accustomed to asking forgiveness instead of permission to obtain information. But with Colt, it would be different.

"Absolutely," Haley assured her, waving to Jackson to join her on the floor even as she kept her dark eyes focused on Sierra. "Just let me know when and if I need to feed him or put him down for a nap?"

"He's already eaten, so he should be happy to play until I return, but if he starts fussing, feel free to see if he wants to lie in his crib."

Arrangements made, Sierra slipped out of the front door a few minutes later. She wore a pair of work boots since the old windmill was a ruin and on a part of the Fenwick property that obviously hadn't been maintained in a long time. At this point, finding a buried diary on this huge property felt like coming up with a needle in a haystack, but she planned to at least try the final structures on her list.

Maybe the reason she hadn't shared the search with Colt was that she didn't really believe she'd find the diary in the first place, even though Emmalou Hilliard had sworn it existed. But still, Sierra hoped. Now more than ever, she wanted to understand Violetta's choices. Her own life had paralleled the woman's in some ways. Maybe whatever the diary had to say about Violetta's decision to live by herself—on her own terms—would help Sierra figure out her next move with Colt.

She unzipped her jacket after the first ten minutes of walking had warmed her up. Using her phone's GPS to ensure she stayed on track as she hiked through an overgrown section of a creek bank, Sierra spotted the stones of the crumbling windmill and hurried the rest of the way to reach it.

Patches of sunlight filtered through the leaves of small scrub trees growing on a hill behind the fallen mill. She had to pick her way over some of the loose limestone blocks now covered with dirt and moss. Yet somehow, the stone base still held the blades in place. Even now, they turned slowly in the breeze while small birds darted back and forth to their nests in two of the hollowed-out spots where stones were missing.

The spot was picturesque despite the decay, new life taking root in the old. Even though the presence of nests made it that much more difficult for her to search those crevices for a diary.

Sighing, she went around to the back of the windmill, looking for the bigger crack she'd seen in the limestone in the pictures she'd viewed online. Sure enough, there it was, centered down the back of the post, the separation larger than it had appeared in the photo.

Still, it remained narrow enough that no bird had tried to nest there, making it easier for Sierra to start her search there. She slipped a pair of thin work gloves from her pocket and slid them on, unwilling to stick her hands into dark places without at least some layer of protection.

"Here goes nothing," she muttered, bracing herself for whatever might be within the stone.

Did snakes nest in rocks like this?

Her nerve almost failed her. But she closed her eyes and reached between the parted limestone blocks. Tapping. Rubbing.

Feeling.

Mostly, there were little bits of crumbled stone and dead leaves. A few sticks, almost as if a bird had tried to build there unsuccessfully. She reached deeper.

And her fingers collided with a straight edge.

Like a tool of some sort, maybe? Or was it just a windmill part? It was definitely a lighter metal and not stone.

Excitement made her stand taller on her toes so she could reach farther into the crevice. Awkwardly, she tried sliding the object toward her with her fingertips. Her gloves slipped off it twice before shifting it a little the third time.

Then, finally, she could edge her thumb beneath it to lift the piece.

The object didn't feel like a book. It felt like a case. But could it contain the diary?

With some twisting and wriggling, she managed to bring out a dusty gray tin—larger than a recipe box, but smaller than a bread box—into the light. The container was rusted in places, but it had been painted at one time. Flecks of red and yellow were still visible around the sides of the lid.

Could this be it?

Sierra kept her gloves on to pry off the top. A piece of rust bit into her finger anyhow, but she ignored the small sting to open the container.

Inside, a dust-covered, warped leather book nestled in dirty cloth that might have once served as a wrapping. A piece of twine held the book shut. But the cover was all that Sierra needed to see. Because even through the collected dust and deteriorated rags, she could read what someone had carefully inscribed with leatherworking tools.

Between two sunflowers, the name Violetta filled her with wonder at the discovery.

She knew that the answers to Violetta's story would be inside this volume, and at last, Sierra's search for answers about the spinster rebel would come to a close. But even as she looked forward to writing the ending to Violetta's tale, Sierra knew that it was the ending to her own, too. With this discovery, she couldn't afford to remain at the Fenwick house anymore.

In order to protect her heart—and ensure she didn't hurt Micah with an even more painful breakup down the road—she needed to leave.

Twelve

After finishing up his meeting with the Wine and Roses Festival coordinator at the Texas Cattleman's Clubhouse that afternoon, Colt strode out of the private meeting room and into the dining hall. Thank goodness Sierra had convinced him to attend to the business in person.

He'd missed this place.

From the oversized leather furniture to the hunting trophies and historical artifacts that decorated the walls, everything about the Texas Cattleman's Club reminded him of home. A member couldn't walk through the place without seeing half a dozen friends. It sure made Colt wonder how his grandfather could have longed for a winery on the other side of the world when Clyde Black had the TCC in his backyard.

Like now, for instance. At the bar, Colt spotted Carson Wentworth sharing a drink with Drake Rhodes. As much as Colt looked forward to returning home to be with Sierra—she'd seemed distracted over breakfast, and he wanted to be certain that didn't have anything to do with their night together—he needed to speak to Carson in person. Sierra had helped him see how important his renovation of the Fenwick property was to a lot of people in Royal. There was a history there, and a lot of it was tied to the Wentworth family. He wanted a way to acknowledge that to Carson.

Heading in the other man's direction, Colt hadn't even reached his side when Carson lifted his beer in salute.

"I'd heard you were back in Royal," Carson greeted him as Colt drew nearer. "Welcome home."

"Thank you." Colt shook hands with both of them before turning his attention to Carson. "And congratulations on your new title. I hear you beat out some stiff competition in your run for TCC president."

Carson had been in a close contest for the president's seat against Lana Langley, the same woman he'd proposed to after the race was over. The other men both laughed, but Carson's green eyes took on a fond light—the half-dazed expression of a man newly in love—before he answered. "Lucky for me, the real prize came later."

Beside Colt, Drake clapped Carson on the shoulder before standing.

"Good to see you, Colt," Drake said as he retrieved his black Stetson from a nearby stool. "And I'm sorry to run, but I promised Cammie I'd join her for a fundraising event she's chairing this afternoon. This one is a fun run and not a gala, so at least I'll be wearing sneakers instead of a tux."

"Give her my best," Colt said as he flagged the bartender to gesture for a beer of his own. "And let her know Micah is growing bigger by the minute."

Drake nodded. "Sierra has been great about visits, texting us updates and sharing photos of Micah. It's really helped Cammie ease away from the big role she played in his life the last few months."

Colt owed Sierra a staggering debt for what she'd done for him. He'd told her as much from the beginning for her role in reuniting him with Micah. But now that he knew her well, he appreciated all she'd done for him even more.

Colt barely managed to stifle a wince at the gut punch of remembering how far he had fallen short in his duties as a father. Even now that he'd assumed responsibility for his son, Sierra was still helping him more than he'd realized, maintaining the connections that Micah's arrival in Royal had forged. Her big heart and caring nature were evident in everything she did. And she sure as hell deserved a family of her own one day.

Was he keeping her from finding that happiness when he wasn't sure how to make a relationship between them work? He hated that idea even as it killed him to think of her with anyone else.

As Drake left them, Colt refocused on Carson. Lowering himself into the seat Drake had vacated, Colt accepted a longneck bottle the bartender handed him. He needed to get home soon and figure things out with Sierra. But first, he wanted to follow through on an offer to the Wentworth family.

"I've been meaning to speak with you, Carson." Colt took a swig of the locally brewed craft beer. "You know I've done extensive renovations on the old Fenwick house."

Carson gave a wave to another rancher taking a seat at the other end of the bar before speaking. "I'd heard as much. Now that we know about Violetta's connection to our family, I'm glad her ranch is being well-maintained."

"Sierra is writing a book about Violetta and the history of the Texas Cattleman's Club. I have the feeling the project will bring about more interest in the ranch." He'd considered the idea of selling the property once he'd renovated the rest, but now he wasn't so sure. Sierra's interest in the Fenwick place—and Violetta—had given him a new appreciation of the ranch's local significance. "Which is why I've been meaning to speak to you."

Carson raised an eyebrow, pausing as he picked up his glass. "I'm listening."

"I hoped you might name the stables once I have them finished. I would take care of the signage and a plaque to honor the history of the place. But I'd like to leave the naming to you, so you could recognize Violetta and Dean or the Wentworths in general?"

Carson set his beer back on the coaster, never having taken a sip. He scrubbed a hand along his jaw, seeming to take in the request. After a moment, he exhaled a long breath.

"That would be much appreciated, Colt." He pushed aside his empty glass. "I'd be honored to name the stables, though I'd like to consult with Harmon first. I know he'll be as pleased as I am that you want to do this."

"It seems only right." The matter settled, Colt caught up on a few other pieces of news from around the TCC, including the lowdown on the other vendors participating in the Wine and Roses event next weekend.

But in the back of his mind, he thought about Sierra and how much of an effect she'd had on his life since he'd returned to Royal. Connecting him with Micah had been huge, of course. But there'd been so many other ways she'd made an indelible mark on his life. Without her, would anyone even know about Violetta Ford? Sierra had jumped into Arielle Martin's work with both feet, picking up where Arielle had left off and doing a lot of good for Royal.

And what had the town given her in return?

He felt a moment's regret that he hadn't talked to her about doing a final story on Micah for the local paper, where she still freelanced. He'd been so convinced she was only in town to dredge up scandal, but he couldn't have been more wrong. She'd done so much for him. He couldn't help thinking he hadn't been an equal partner. He needed to make things right between them before he left Royal.

So, finishing his beer, he shook hands with Carson and headed for the door. He needed to return home and see Sierra. He'd find out the reason for her distracted air over breakfast, and then do whatever he could to fix it. Because he wanted her to remain in his life for as long as he was in town.

And maybe even after he returned.

Sierra had made him see that he and Micah belonged in Royal. So his upcoming trip to France didn't need to be permanent. He could finish his work at the winery there, then bring Micah home to start a branch of the Royal Black Winery here.

For the first time in a long time, he felt the stirrings of hope. And he couldn't wait to share that with her.

* * *

Pulling clothes off the hangers and folding them in her bedroom at the Fenwick house, Sierra heard Colt's foot on the staircase.

Her stomach cramped at the sound. Just days ago, she would have felt a thrill at the prospect of seeing him, even if she hadn't wanted to admit it to herself.

Now, after knowing how deeply she'd begun to care for him and how much damage that could do to her relationship with Micah, Sierra felt only anxiety. Dread. A sickness at what she was about to do.

Because she knew, without a doubt, he wouldn't understand her decision.

Clearing out the middle drawer of a built-in bureau inside the massive walk-in closet, she didn't bother folding her night clothes or active wear. She just chucked the untidy pile into the suitcase on top of the few dress clothes she'd brought with her.

That's how Colt found her when he walked into the room, her hands smoothing out the pile enough so she could fasten the elastic strap to hold the clothes in place inside her luggage. She sensed his presence behind her even before she turned around.

The air shifted somehow, all her nerve endings attuned to this man who'd grown to mean a great deal to her in a short span of time.

"Sierra?"

Biting her lip, she didn't need to turn and see his

expression to read into his tone of voice. Surprise. Wariness. Cautious concern.

She heard all of that and more in the space of a single word.

"How was your meeting at the TCC?" she asked carefully, trying to keep her own voice neutral. The last thing she wanted was to fall apart in front of him. It wouldn't make any difference in the outcome of their talk anyhow. "Did you straighten out the wine shipments?"

"It went well. The Royal Black wines will arrive in time for the festival. Is Micah still sleeping?" He walked closer, the soft sound of his footfalls on the hardwood floor making her realize that he'd removed his boots when he'd entered the house.

Such an unremarkable detail to notice when things were about to crumble between them. But she couldn't help thinking of the intimacy they shared that went beyond the bedroom. There were a hundred details she'd learned about Colt by living with him these last weeks. The way he liked his coffee in the morning. That he woke up without an alarm when the sun rose. That he moved with athletic grace for someone his size, his step almost silent as he came up beside her now. She would miss all those things, and so much more.

"He is out like a light. Haley and Jackson visited with him today, and he's all tired out from playing." She closed the lid of her soft-sided suitcase, her fingers shaking a little as she reached for the zipper. "I'm glad you were able to settle things at the Texas Cattleman's Club."

"Sierra, what's going on?" He covered her hand with his, halting her before she could close the case. "Why are you packing?"

The warmth of his touch slid right past her defenses, reminding her how easy it would be to lean into his strength. To let their attraction burn away all the difficult parts of their relationship. But for how long?

Even if she allowed that to happen, they'd be right back to this point tomorrow.

Taking a deep breath, she moved away from him. Not just because his touch was so potent, she told herself. She also wanted to show him the diary.

Retrieving the leather volume from the low mahogany desk near the guest bed that had been hers the last two weeks, she passed it to him. His blue eyes were full of concern as he looked at her, and she wished she could capture the moment since she suspected he wouldn't be so pleased with her when he found out she'd been searching for the diary all along.

"I found this hidden in the old windmill today," she explained after his gaze shifted down to the object in his hands. "It's Violetta Ford's diary."

His brow furrowed as he turned it over, examining the worn book. Her attention narrowed to his hands. She was going to miss his touch so much. The sound of his voice. Why hadn't she considered that more before she let herself get so attached to him?

"I don't understand. What were you doing at the windmill? The property is in shambles over there." He lifted his eyes to her face again, and for a moment, the concern lingered. "I'm not sure it's a safe place for walking the baby—"

All at once, his expression cleared, the confusion morphing into understanding briefly before suspicion took its place.

"You went there looking for this," he said flatly, his grip tightening around the leather. His left jaw muscle ticked. "It only makes sense since you're researching a book on Violetta that you would welcome the chance to search the property for clues about her. Cammie did tell me that you didn't stop until you had answers."

"I think Violetta's story is worth documenting. Both as a woman and as a TCC member," she rushed to explain, feeling defensive. She'd had more time to consider the local spinster rebel, and the more Sierra thought about her, the more she found to admire. "She refused to compromise the kind of life she wanted for the sake of social norms. She was a frontier maverick, a woman unafraid to take chances."

Colt's face had turned stony. "She also abandoned her baby," he reminded her.

Did he dare to imply Sierra was abandoning Micah, too? Whether or not that had been his intention, he certainly knew the topic would be sensitive for her. His words struck her every last frustrated maternal nerve.

"In those days, she knew her child would be labeled illegitimate, and that would limit his chances in life," she found herself arguing, having read some of the diary already. She couldn't help herself, even though she knew the book was technically Colt's property now since it had been discovered on his land. "She loved him too much for that. Instead, she gave him up to be raised in a life of luxury by his dad, Dean Wentworth."

Slowly, Colt placed the diary on top of Sierra's suitcase, setting the luggage aside.

"So you've been searching for the diary the whole time." His blue eyes sparked with fire as he met her gaze again. "It doesn't feel good to think that might have been your real reason for being here. Would you have even said yes to the nanny position if it hadn't been for the chance to explore the Fenwick land?"

She hesitated, knowing there was some truth to what he said. But it was only a small part of her reason.

"You can't possibly question how much I love Micah," she flashed back at him. "I wanted to spend time with him, and I'm fortunate you gave me the chance to do that. This has nothing to do with him."

"And yet I noticed you're packing your bags the moment the diary came to light." He made a sweeping gesture around the guest room, where some of Sierra's belongings were still scattered. "That tells me you were more interested in your professional search for answers than you were in Micah." He paused a moment before adding, more quietly, "Or me."

The fact she might have hurt him by leaving hadn't occurred to her. Something twisted in her chest. Her instinct was to reach out to him. Touch him. But hadn't he made it clear that they didn't have a future? She stuffed her hands in the pockets of her jeans.

"You've said all along you don't want a relationship. You told me from the beginning that you're returning to France and taking Micah with you." A thready panic loosed inside her. Had she misread the situation?

Had there been a time when he'd thought about something more between them, and she'd missed the chance to explore these tumultuous feelings?

But that was foolish to think. He'd been on a collision course with his destiny at Royal Black Winery since they met.

"So you gladly made your time here about work

instead of…whatever we shared." He didn't budge an inch, keeping his distance from her.

She bristled, immediately defensive. So much for letting her guard down.

"That's not fair. I heard you tell Micah that very first day not to get too attached to me. That I was temporary." She remembered overhearing those words before she stepped into the nursery to check on him. "And I understand that, Colt. Your first obligation is your son, and it makes sense that you want to protect him. That's why I'm leaving. It's easier to end things now before we get even more attached. I don't want to hurt Micah more down the road."

"So your answer is to run?" His voice lowered. He stretched his strong arms wide in disbelief. "How can you think that's a good plan after everything you said about Micah needing to be around people he's bonded with? You came here so he'd have someone familiar around him. Doesn't that matter anymore?"

Was she making a mistake?

The confusion in his voice, the indignation at her decision, made her question herself. But he'd been so quick to jump to conclusions about her search for the diary, not giving her the benefit of the doubt. How could she be with someone who just assumed the worst of her? If she didn't stick to her path—maintaining her focus on her career—

she'd only run into the same hurts that had almost leveled her four years ago when she discovered she wouldn't have children. It was one thing for her to make peace with not having kids. But she couldn't be responsible for someone else grappling with the reality of that.

"*You* are familiar to Micah now," she reminded him, blinking past the burning feeling in her eyes. "You've read him bedtime stories and kissed him good-night. Fed him and changed him and rocked him in your arms at night." Her voice faltered at the memory of Colt staring down into the crib the night before, awed at the responsibility of raising his son. "Micah has you."

Reminded how tough it would be to walk out of this house today, Sierra picked up another duffel bag and brought it over to the desk to pack her work things.

"You're just scared," Colt accused a moment later, his voice cool now. Dispassionate.

Of course he was right.

She was terrified of losing Micah. And yes, Colt, too. But the longer she stayed, the worse it would hurt. Dragging in a breath, she waited to speak until she trusted her voice to remain even.

"Says the man who's moving to France." She zipped the second bag shut and hefted the weight onto her shoulder, adjusting the strap. "I guess that makes two of us."

For a moment, Colt looked like he was wrestling with what to say next. Part of her wished he would tell her differently. That she had it all wrong. That he wasn't moving, and that he wanted to try out a life together with her.

Or maybe she just wanted to hear that it was okay she couldn't have children, whispered a tiny piece of her heart that she chose to ignore.

But when Colt spoke again, he was all business.

"I'm not going to let you carry your own bags," he said finally, lifting the wide strap of the duffel off of her shoulder.

His knuckles brushed her arm as he took the weight, sending an unwanted shiver through her. Memories of so many other touches taunted her. But his face was a cool mask now, all hint of concern long gone.

Not trusting herself to speak, she simply nodded while he set aside the forgotten diary and lifted her suitcase from the bed.

Her attention remained fixed on the leather volume for a long moment. Even while her heart broke, she couldn't help but give some thought to Violetta, the woman whose unconventional journey had inspired Sierra over the last five months.

"What will you do with the diary?" she asked. "I'm sure Harmon would like to hear Violetta loved him. It's an artifact that would be of interest to any local historian."

He looked at her long and hard, his eyes grown cool as the gulf between them widened.

"You're the one writing the book on Violetta and the TCC. It's probably of most interest to you." Standing on the threshold of the guest room door with her bags, he turned to look back at her. "Take it. But when you're finished, the diary should probably go to Harmon. Let him decide what to do with it next. Family is what really matters, after all."

She felt raw inside, like he'd raked over all her feelings and found her wanting. Family mattered to her, too. But she had never been a part of his, even if some days it had felt like she belonged here, with him and with Micah. Swallowing back the bitterness of the hurt, she tried to focus on the gift he'd offered her.

If her work was all she had, at least the diary would make it easier to write her book.

"Thank you," she said softly, picking up the slim volume, mindful of its age.

But Colt was already gone, his footfalls heavier on the stairs now that he carried her bags than when he'd first arrived in her room. Not that she was surprised that her baggage was weighty. Unwieldy.

Following him out, she clutched the diary to her chest, wishing the historic book was enough of a prize to soothe her broken heart.

Thirteen

The weather for the Wine and Roses Festival proved ideal, with clear skies and sunshine that showcased the local gardens at their best. Everyone commented on it as they stopped by Colt's wine tasting booth in the gardens outside of the Texas Cattleman's Club. Colt knew he should be celebrating the successful event.

But no amount of sunny weather could dissipate the dark cloud that still hung stubbornly over his head a week after Sierra had left him. He'd swung from hurt to angry at first. But as the days ticked by, he realized that underneath that, he was just plain devastated.

He nodded at Nathan and Amanda Battle as the couple walked by, though Colt kept moving to minimize conversation when he knew he wasn't at his best. Today was a triumph for Royal Black Winery, with orders piling up from local tasters. People didn't just ask for a bottle. They bought by the case. The show of support from Royal was overwhelming, and Colt knew he should be thrilled. Certainly he was happy for his grandfather's sake that so many people remembered him well and were excited to be a part of Clyde's dream. And yet without Sierra at his side, sharing this with him, the day still felt empty.

He glanced back at the clubhouse building, grateful he hadn't needed to bring Micah to the day care facility. He'd ended up hiring Katie-Lynn, the nanny candidate Sierra had liked best for Micah, and the woman had been more than competent.

Colt supposed he should have been happy that he'd found someone trustworthy who Micah liked. But that proved tough when he missed everything about Sierra, including the way she was with his son.

Now, with a country band playing a lively zydeco waltz on the opposite end of the pool from his booth, Colt tried to scavenge up his game face as more people filtered into the event. He recognized Carson Wentworth's fiancée, Lana Langley, and Lana's sister-in-law, Abigail Langley Price, as the women stopped in front of his display. They examined the wine bottles on the table and read the six-foot banner about the French winery with the Royal name. The event company he'd hired to help him design a presence for Royal Black had done a good job for his debut on U.S. soil.

The Wine and Roses Festival lasted all day at different venues around town, including the Cimarron Rose B and B where he happened to know Sierra was once again staying. Not that he'd driven past it a few times this week like a lovestruck kid, hoping to see her. Needing to figure out how the hell things had gone so wrong between them. Wishing he could wind back time and somehow fix things.

Abigail faced Colt now that she and Lana had finished browsing the display. Her long red hair fell forward as she bent to choose one of the tasting cups on the table, her expression thoughtful as she selected a vintage to sip. Beside her, dark-haired Lana worked more methodically, trying the three available wines in order. The contrast in their styles made Colt think of him and Sierra—Colt quietly cautious, Sierra charging forward.

Was there anything that *didn't* make him think of her lately?

"Wow. This is fantastic, Colt," Abigail declared a moment later as she lifted the vineyard's signature bottle, the Malbec, examining the label before meeting his eyes. "Your grandfather would be so proud of you."

"Thank you, Abby. Granddad would have loved the winery." He told himself that he should discuss the wine. That was his job today, after all. But after a week without Sierra, he found he didn't have the heart for small talk when Abby might know something about the woman he'd been missing for days. "Did I, uh, hear right that Sierra will be speaking tonight?"

He'd heard that she planned to share snippets from Violetta Ford's diary in relation to the TCC. The club's Women's Association had organized a reading during the Roses Under the Stars dinner that capped the Wine and Roses Festival since Violetta had become something of a cult hero to the female membership. In her guise as Vincent Fenwick, Violetta had been the first woman member, technically ousting Abigail for that honor.

There must have been something peculiar about his tone of voice, because Lana's ears seemed to prick up, and she moved closer to join their discussion. Abby's reaction was subtler, but there was no mistaking the curiosity in her blue eyes.

"Sierra is scheduled to say a few words about Violetta's diary for the Women's Association tonight," Abby informed him before passing her credit card to one of his booth assistants, indicating that she wanted two cases of the Malbec. "I imagine she'll be here soon. When Lana and I saw her at the Cimarron Rose, she had just come into the rose garden. And she was already dressed for dinner."

Anticipation fired through him. Colt remembered his first meeting with her in that rose garden, sharing a bench with her as she tried to explain to how she'd connected Arielle's diary to him. He'd been upset, jet-lagged, and beside himself about leaving a child on the opposite side of the Atlantic from him. Yet even then, he'd felt the pull toward Sierra, the dynamo who hadn't let an obstacle like an ocean get in the way of her quest for answers.

Damn it, he missed her so much. Every second of every day and night, he wanted her by his side.

As he was jostled from behind, he recognized he'd never answered Abby when Lana edged closer still to add, "Sierra told us how you let her borrow Violetta's diary for research purposes. That was very kind of you, Colt, since we're all eager to learn more about one of Royal's feisty females."

His throat burned with regret to think Sierra had been speaking so well of him, crediting him with the diary somehow when he'd done nothing but give her a hard time about searching for it. Even though he'd known all along it was her job to dig for answers.

Her special gift as a person.

Why had he insisted on seeing that skill as negative? Not all investigative reporters were out to raise scandal for the fun of it.

It's the Royal Gazette, *not* TMZ, she'd told him when they first met, back when he'd been convinced she wanted to write a story about how he'd left Arielle Martin pregnant and alone while he founded a French winery. But she'd never done anything of the sort. His view of the media had been skewed a long time ago, after his parents' deaths, and he'd never bothered trying to see a member of the press in a different light. That was on him.

"Sierra did all the leg work," he admitted finally, realizing his preoccupation amounted to rudeness to two important local ladies who were trying to support his business. With an effort, he tried to shake off the dark cloud over his head for the hundredth time that day. "She searched the property for the diary with Micah while taking care of him during the day, then worked on her book at night."

Abby and Lana exchanged a look before Lana smiled at him.

"Multitasking is sort of a feminine superpower." She mimed shining her nails on the label of her red dress styled like a long men's jacket. "In fact, Sierra said something about her work slowing down since she stopped taking care of Micah. I'll bet she misses him."

He wondered if she felt half as hollow inside as he did this week. But he understood maybe that was his perfect excuse to speak to her. Surely she wanted to arrange a visit with Micah in the upcoming days? She hadn't seen him for a whole week. Already he found himself searching the festival crowd for any sign of Sierra's blond hair.

Abigail signed the receipt for her wine and took possession of her credit card again before saying, "Sierra also told us you were returning to France soon."

His head whipped around to meet Abby's gaze. He wanted to ask her for every detail that Sierra had shared, he was so starved for news of her. Instead, he explained, "I haven't firmed up my plans yet. I still have a lot to settle here."

And how strange that was since he'd been so eager to return home. Now he was dragging his feet, his plans on idle since his breakup. He'd wanted to make things right with her a whole week ago—after he'd come home from his talk with Carson Wentworth. Even then, he'd wanted to talk to her about getting together again once he returned to Royal. But his plans had gone up in smoke when he'd come home that day and found her packing her things.

Just the sight of her with a suitcase in her hand had sent his thoughts off the rails. And then he'd jumped on the first cause for blame he could find. Her search for the diary.

"Well, I can't help but hope that once you settle things here, you'll realize how much you'll miss Royal if you leave us again." Abby tucked her receipt in her red leather purse and closed the clasp on her bag. "The Blacks are a Royal family."

Lana tapped one of his wine bottles with a long pink fingernail. "It says so right on the label. And Micah is kind of a native son after the way the town rallied around him." A smile curved her lips. "Do you know how many of us were ready to adopt him? I would have stood in line myself to be a volunteer mama, except I don't think I could take on Cammie Wentworth."

For the first time since he'd returned to Royal, he didn't feel the same twinge of guilt that he usually experienced about abandoning his child by not having followed up after the brief affair. Hearing Lana talk about how Royal embraced Micah helped Colt see how quickly his hometown had been ready to come to the boy's rescue. How many places could boast the small-town feel that Royal had always possessed? He would offer to stay here if that made a difference to Sierra. Because Royal was a place to call home.

As the gardens and pool area outside the TCC filled with people tasting local wines and dancing to the country band, Colt still scanned the grounds, hoping for a sight of Sierra. He needed to try one more time to fix things.

To be a better man for her.

"Micah is a charmer," Colt acknowledged, seized with a new sense of purpose now. The dark cloud over his head hadn't left, but maybe there was still a chance he could salvage something from the ruins of his relationship with Sierra. "And I'll always be grateful to everyone who was ready to help Micah. But there's only one reason I would stay in Royal, and I'm not sure if she still wants me."

Abby Langley Price seemed to be fighting to hide a smile as she said, "You'll have to ask her." Then she nodded toward someone behind him.

Pivoting fast, he caught sight of Sierra entering the garden area from the clubhouse, a fitted black dress skimming her curves. The high neck and long length were demure, but a high slit at the thigh and slashes in the fabric along her shoulders made the dress sexy.

No. It was the woman inside the gown that did that part.

"Sierra?" His voice rasped as if the word was unfamiliar to him.

She wasn't close enough to hear him, yet somehow she must have sensed his notice, because she turned toward him suddenly, green eyes meeting his from twenty yards away.

He hoped Abby and Lana weren't offended, but he couldn't take his eyes off Sierra. He needed to speak to her. "Ladies, I hope you'll excuse me."

Fueled with a new determination, he charged toward Sierra. Because he couldn't move on with his life until he told her how much he missed her. How much he loved her.

He hadn't wanted to admit it, even to himself, for fear he'd mess up his life plan and the commitment he'd made to his grandfather's memory. But in his heart, he knew his grandfather would never want him to sacrifice his future for the sake of a winery.

He just hoped it wasn't too late to make Sierra see that they were meant for each other. Because he loved her more than he could have imagined possible.

And he hoped like hell she felt the same.

* * *

Why did she have to turn and meet Colt Black's eyes the moment she stepped out into the gardens behind the Texas Cattleman's Club? There must have been two hundred people out there, milling around the booths and listening to the country band.

Two hundred people, and Sierra just happened to lock eyes with Colt. It made no sense that something could feel so improbable and yet inevitable at the same time.

Of course, she'd torn her attention away as fast as possible, but even that had been like slow motion since she'd missed the sight of him. Now she gathered her skirt in her hands and headed in the opposite direction, hardly seeing where she was going until she reached an archway of pink roses that ended in a small bench tucked off to one side. There was no exit. And no people, either, to help her make an escape or at least pretend to exchange small talk as a buffer.

She must have walked beyond the festival area without really seeing. But then, turning on one black peau de soie heel to backtrack, she all but ran into a wall masquerading as a man's chest.

"Oof." She made an inelegant noise as she half bounced off the muscular wall. A pair of strong masculine hands reached to steady her.

The scent of pine and sandalwood told her who she'd run into even before she picked her chin up to meet a familiar pair of cobalt-blue eyes. Her breath hitched in her throat. All the loneliness of the past week without him came swelling back to the fore, the ache, the regret.

But he was here. Now. He looked so handsome in his evening wear. The Roses Under the Stars dinner didn't call for a tux, but his black suit was almost as formal. Clean-shaven and hair freshly trimmed, Colt appeared ready for the next phase of the evening.

Did he have a date? The possibility made her stomach hurt and her heart break all over again.

"I'm sorry, Sierra." Colt's words wrapped around her even as his hands fell away from her shoulders. "I didn't mean to startle you. I was trying to get your attention."

Had he called to her? Her thoughts had been so full of trying to escape attention that she might not have heard. Now she could hear the country band switching to a slower waltz. Fairy lights began to come on around the gardens, a reminder that her presentation would start shortly. Still, the evening was so lovely, she was in no rush to retreat indoors.

"It's fine." She stretched her lips in what she hoped passed for a polite smile, still thinking about the possibility of him bringing a date to the evening festivities. "I'm all right. What do you need? Is Micah all right?"

"Micah's fine," he reassured her quickly, then cupped her arm gently in his broad, strong hand. "Can I talk to you for a few minutes? I know you have an obligation to speak soon, but we still have a little time." He pointed to his watch even though she was well aware of the hour.

"I came out here to keep from getting nervous about, uh, presenting about Violetta's diary," she blurted, unsure how he would feel about her presenting to the group about the small volume she'd found. Had he forgiven her for searching for it? "I thought the fresh air would help."

"Then do you mind if we sit for a while?" He gestured toward the wooden bench under the arbor. "I'll help you keep track of the hour."

Her heart thundered. She could have sworn it felt like an incoming storm inside her chest with all the rumbling. He didn't look angry at all. Could he have rethought his position on the diary?

On the two of them?

But if so, why hadn't he so much as called her this week? In order to have closure, she needed the answer to that, either way.

"I suppose that would be all right," she agreed finally, giving a jerky nod and allowing him to lead her toward the bench.

She'd forgotten how nice it felt to have his hands on her. Just the smallest brush of his fingertips on her lower back made her feel weak.

A burst of laughter from the festival area reminded Sierra that other people were still mingling close by even though their corner nook among the roses felt very private. The scent would forever remind her of this moment with Colt.

Lowering herself onto the wooden bench, she tried to keep a reasonable amount of space between them without looking like she was avoiding him. But the thought of him touching her again made her hyperconscious of her body. She couldn't afford to melt at his feet.

"I've missed you," he began without preamble, surprising her with his directness. "More than I can say."

What? Had she misheard? For a moment, she wondered if the heady scent of the roses had somehow made her light-headed, because heaven help her, she'd missed him more than she could have imagined possible. She hadn't known it was possible to care so much for one person. To love one person so much.

"I—" She stalled, unsure how to respond to his statement—the very last thing she would have expected him to say. She'd been prepared for his anger. Not this. Backtracking, she couldn't help but ask, "You do?"

He shook his head his voice sounding strained. "That you'd doubt it for a minute lets me know how much I've failed you."

Out of her depth, she allowed herself to study him more carefully. She hadn't noticed the dark smudges beneath his eyes earlier when they'd locked gazes. But even in the shadowed nook, she could see them now. Had sleep eluded him, too?

Had their argument kept him awake all night the way it had her this whole week?

"I don't understand." She licked her lips, telling herself to keep her hopes in check. Just because he said he missed her didn't mean that anything else had changed. "I've missed you, too, but I know that you're still leaving Royal. And I know that I will remain focused on my career while I try and make peace with my...fertility problems."

That old hurt hadn't gone away. She wasn't ready to share it with anyone else. Especially after what happened between her and Colt.

He picked up her hand from where it rested on the bench. He layered it carefully between both of his. What was it about him that made her feel so cherished? So special? Her eyes burned at the knowledge that she might never feel this way with anyone else ever again.

"If you've missed me the way I've missed you, I think we can work things out. Because we care about one another deeply." He squeezed her palm.

"I care about you. So much. But—"

"No buts. Let's think through this, because I know I would compromise a whole lot to be together again." His voice was strong, sure. Though she could see the vulnerability in his eyes. "For starters, I don't need to go to France unless you want to go with me. I'll let you make the call."

She straightened in her seat, wondering how else he might surprise her. "I'd go to France in a heartbeat and write travel articles if you wanted me there, but that doesn't change the bigger issue."

She felt nervous now, sensing the next topic up for discussion. She wasn't sure she could have remained seated if he hadn't been holding on to her hand and looking in her eyes the way he might gentle a scared horse.

"There's nothing to discuss," she reminded him, trying to keep her voice steady. "Mine isn't a problem that anyone can fix."

"Then maybe you shouldn't look at it as a problem that needs fixing, Sierra." He curled her palm inside his and lifted his other hand to her face, stroking her cheek with his thumb. "I love you. Every single thing about you, I love. And there's no part of you that I'd change, because then you wouldn't be the uniquely incredible woman that you are."

A half sob escaped her throat midway through his words. She had to cover her lips to keep in the rest of the emotion ready to burst free.

"You have to know you're incredible and I, uh, care for you so very much," she confessed, a tear spilling from one eye. "But how can you be sure you love me?"

"Love defies logic. There's no way I can prove

my feelings for you, except with time," he protested, thumbing away the tear. "But make no mistake, it's the truth. I couldn't even function this week without you in my life. I just had a conversation with two women at my booth who wanted to buy wine, but I couldn't even dredge up a single interesting thing to say about the Malbec when I only wanted to ask them questions about you."

A small laugh escaped her. How easy would it be to fall into his arms and absorb all that love shining from his words, from his eyes?

"I haven't thought of anything but you and Micah either." She tipped her face into his hand, savoring the feeling of his fingertips on her temple after not being near him all week. She drew in a deep breath and shared the words she'd sworn she would never utter to another person again. "I love you, too, with my whole heart. And because I love you, I don't want you to be hurt. How can you know how you'll feel about a life with no more children in ten years from now? What if you regret—"

Softly, he kissed her lips, quieting her question. Then, while fireflies danced behind her eyelids, he spoke against her lips.

"Please give me credit for knowing my own heart." He kissed her once more, and she opened her eyes to meet his steady blue gaze. "For knowing what I want. You're it for me, Sierra. If I can't have you, there will be no more children ten years from now anyway, because I will have missed out on the only woman I want to be Micah's mother."

There was something so unflinching in the way he said it that allowed her to feel how much he meant it. That helped her see how much he loved her.

The sob in her throat this time was all happy. And she did fling herself right into his arms. Wrapped him up tight.

"I love you so much, Colt. You're it for me, too. Always."

She clung to him shamelessly, not caring if her outfit wrinkled, if her mascara smeared, or if her hair ended up in a tangled mess. Soon she'd have to speak to the Texas Cattleman's Club, and she'd surely look like a hot mess. But the residents of Royal, Texas, already knew she cared more about a good story than looking like a beauty queen.

And her story just got an ending better than she could have ever imagined with the man of her dreams.

* * * * *

Look for a brand new
Texas Cattleman's Club series,
Ranchers and Rivals, available next month!

Staking a Claim
by USA TODAY bestselling author
Janice Maynard

#2869 STAKING A CLAIM

Texas Cattleman's Club: Ranchers and Rivals • by Janice Maynard

With dreams of running the family ranch, Layla Grandin has no time for matchmaking. Then, set up with a reluctant date, Layla realizes he sent his twin instead! Their attraction is undeniable but, when the ranch is threatened, can she afford distractions?

#2870 LOST AND FOUND HEIR

Dynasties: DNA Dilemma • by Joss Wood

Everything is changing for venture capitalist Garrett Kaye—he's now the heir to a wealthy businessman *and* the company's next CEO. But none of this stops him from connecting with headstrong Jules Carson. As passions flare, will old wounds and new revelations derail everything?

#2871 MONTANA LEGACY

by Katie Frey

After the loss of his brother, rancher Nick Hartmann is suddenly the guardian of his niece. Enter Rose Kelly—the new tutor. Sparks fly, but with his ranch at stake and the secrets she's keeping, there's a lot at risk for them both...

#2872 ONE NIGHT EXPECTATIONS

Devereaux Inc. • by LaQuette

Successful attorney Amara Devereaux-Rodriguez is focused on closing her family's multibillion dollar deal. But then she meets Lennox Carlisle, the councilman and mayoral candidate who stands in their way. He's hard to resist. And one hot night together leads to a little surprise neither expected...

#2873 BLACK TIE BACHELOR BID

Little Black Book of Secrets • by Karen Booth

To build her boutique hotel, socialite Taylor Klein needs reclusive hotelier Roman Scott—even if that means buying his "date" at a charity bachelor auction. She wins the bid and a night with him, but will the sparks between them upend her goals?

#2874 SECRETS OF A WEDDING CRASHER

Destination Wedding • by Katherine Garbera

Hoping for career advancement, lobbyist Melody Conner crashes a high-profile wedding to meet with Senator Darien Bisset. What she didn't expect was to spend the night with him. There's a chemistry neither can deny, but being together could upend all their professional goals...

HDCNM0322

SPECIAL EXCERPT FROM

(H) HARLEQUIN
DESIRE

*To oust his twin brother from the family company,
CEO Samuel Kane sets him up to break the company's
cardinal rule—no workplace relationships. But it's Samuel
who finds himself tempted when Arlie Banks reawakens
a passion that could cost him everything...*

Read on for a sneak peek at
Corner Office Confessions
by USA TODAY *bestselling author Cynthia St. Aubin.*

A sharp rap on her door startled Arlie out of her misery.

"Just a minute!" she called, twisting off the shower.

Opening the shower door, she slid into one of the complimentary plush robes, then gathered the long skein of her hair and squeezed the water out of it with a towel before draping it over her shoulder.

Good enough for food delivery. She exited the bathroom in a cloud of steam and pulled open the propped door.

Samuel Kane's face appeared in the gap.

Only he didn't look like Samuel Kane.

He looked like wrath in a Brooks Brothers suit. Jaw set, the muscles flexed, mouth a thin, grim line. Eyes blazing emerald against chiseled cheekbones.

"Oh," she said dumbly. "Hi."

A sinking feeling of self-consciousness further heated her already shower-warmed skin as he stared at her.

"Do you want to come in?" she added when he made no reply. She stepped aside to grant him entry, catching the subtle scent of him as he moved past her into the hallway.

"Why didn't you tell me?" he asked.

Arlie's heart sank into her guts. There were too many answers to this question. And too many questions he didn't even know to ask.

"Tell you what?" she asked, opting for the safest path.

Coward.

Samuel stepped closer, her glowing white robe reflected in icy arcs in his glacier-green eyes. "About my father. About what he said to you this morning."

The wave of relief was so complete and acute it actually weakened her knees.

"Our families have a lot of shared history," Arlie said. "Not all of it good."

"He had no right—"

"I'm sorry," she interrupted, knowing it was a weak and deliberate dodge. She didn't want to talk about this. Not with him. "It's absolutely mandatory that you surrender your tie and suit jacket for this conversation. I'm entirely underdressed and frankly feeling a little vulnerable about it."

Walking into the well-appointed sitting area, Samuel shrugged out of his suit jacket and laid it across the chaise longue. As he turned, they snagged gazes. He gripped the knot of his tie, loosening it with small deliberate strokes that inexplicably kindled heat between Arlie's thighs.

"Better?" he asked.

On a different night, in a different universe, it would have ended there.

But for reasons she could neither explain nor ignore, Arlie padded barefoot across the space between them.

"Almost." Lifting her hands to his neck, she undid the button closest to his collar. Then another. And another.

To her great surprise and delight, Samuel wore no T-shirt beneath.

Dizzy with desire, Arlie tilted her face up to his. The air was alive with electricity, crackling and sizzling with anticipation. The breathless inevitability of this thing between them made her feel loose-limbed and drunk.

"All my life, I could have anything I wanted." Cupping her jaw, he ran the pad of his thumb over her lower lip. "Except you."

Arlie's breath came in irregular bursts, something deep inside her tightening at his admission. "You want me?"

Samuel only looked at her, silent but saying all.

His wordlessness the purest part of what he had always given her.

The look that passed between them was both question and answer.

Yes?

Yes.

Don't miss what happens next in...
Corner Office Confessions
by USA TODAY *bestselling author Cynthia St. Aubin.*

Available May 2022 wherever
Harlequin Desire books and ebooks are sold.

Harlequin.com

HDEXP0322

Get 4 FREE REWARDS!

We'll send you 2 FREE Books plus 2 FREE Mystery Gifts.

FREE Value Over $20

Both the **Harlequin® Desire** and **Harlequin Presents®** series feature compelling
novels filled with passion, sensuality and intriguing scandals.

YES! Please send me 2 FREE novels from the Harlequin Desire or Harlequin
Presents series and my 2 FREE gifts (gifts are worth about $10 retail). After
receiving them, if I don't wish to receive any more books, I can return the
shipping statement marked "cancel." If I don't cancel, I will receive 6 brand-new
Harlequin Presents Larger-Print books every month and be billed just $5.80
each in the U.S. or $5.99 each in Canada, a savings of at least 11% off the
cover price or 6 Harlequin Desire books every month and be billed just $4.55
each in the U.S. or $5.24 each in Canada, a savings of at least 13% off the
cover price. It's quite a bargain! Shipping and handling is just 50¢ per book in
the U.S. and $1.25 per book in Canada.* I understand that accepting the 2 free
books and gifts places me under no obligation to buy anything. I can always
return a shipment and cancel at any time. The free books and gifts are mine to
keep no matter what I decide.

Choose one: ☐ **Harlequin Desire**   ☐ **Harlequin Presents Larger-Print**
                  (225/326 HDN GNND)   (176/376 HDN GNWY)

Name (please print)

Address   Apt. #

City   State/Province   Zip/Postal Code

Email: Please check this box ☐ if you would like to receive newsletters and promotional emails from Harlequin Enterprises ULC and
its affiliates. You can unsubscribe anytime.

Mail to the **Harlequin Reader Service:**
IN U.S.A.: P.O. Box 1341, Buffalo, NY 14240-8531
IN CANADA: P.O. Box 603, Fort Erie, Ontario L2A 5X3

Want to try 2 free books from another series? Call 1-800-873-8635 or visit www.ReaderService.com.

Love Harlequin romance?

DISCOVER.

Be the first to find out about promotions, news and exclusive content!

 Facebook.com/HarlequinBooks

 Twitter.com/HarlequinBooks

 Instagram.com/HarlequinBooks

 Pinterest.com/HarlequinBooks

You Tube YouTube.com/HarlequinBooks

ReaderService.com

EXPLORE.

Sign up for the Harlequin e-newsletter and download a free book from any series at **TryHarlequin.com**

CONNECT.

Join our Harlequin community to share your thoughts and connect with other romance readers! **Facebook.com/groups/HarlequinConnection**

HSOCIAL2021